Visit us at www.boldstrokesbooks.com

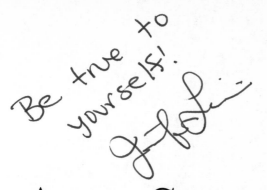

Be true to yourself!

ANDY SQUARED

by

Jennifer Lavoie

A Division of Bold Strokes Books

2012

ANDY SQUARED

ISBN 13: 978-1-60282-743-1

This Trade Paperback Original Is Published By
Bold Strokes Books, Inc.
P.O. Box 249
Valley Falls, NY 12185

First Edition: September 2012

Credits
Editors: Lynda Sandoval and Stacia Seaman
Production Design: Stacia Seaman
Cover Design by Sheri (graphicartist2020@hotmail.com)

Acknowledgments

This book would not be what it is without the help of Mom, Dad, and my sisters, Tiffany and Cassandra. Thank you for dealing with the weird one in the family! My deepest gratitude goes to Dr. Cappella. Without your class and encouragement, this novel might never have seen the light of day. It may have taken years, but I did it! I appreciate my friends and students who read the various drafts and commented kindly but critically. Last, but certainly not least, my wonderful editor, Lynda Sandoval. You rock! I couldn't have asked for a better guide.

For my family and friends who put up with me
while I wrote this.

CHAPTER ONE

The neon yellow ball rolled to a stop in front of Andrew. He leaned over and placed his hands on his knees, panting.

"Again."

"Andrea," he started, pausing to catch his breath. "We're good. We have to get ready for school." He heard a beep and saw the faint blue glow from her watch.

"We have ten minutes," Andrea said, and put her hands on her hips. She stood between two orange cones, ready to defend her position. The harsh light from the barn floodlight lit up her face in the early, pre-dawn morning. She squinted against it and pushed a strand of her blond hair off her forehead.

Andrew groaned and straightened up, settling his foot under the ball and flipping it into the air. He juggled it on his knee for a moment before letting it rest back onto the ground. Why had he insisted on an early-morning practice? He hated mornings, and so did his twin, so why had they been out here since shortly after five thirty, running up and down the small field by the old barn, with Andrea pushing him like a drill sergeant? Because he'd missed the easiest goal at the last game. The keeper ran out of his box and left the net wide open, and Andrew missed. *What an idiot.*

He scowled at the ball and kicked it forward, dribbling it down the field toward Andrea. She moved her hands from her hips and crouched down, holding them in front of her.

"Focus, Andy," she yelled. "Don't think about that goal, just do it. It's all over your face. You're gonna freeze up if you keep thinking about it!"

Easier said than done, he thought, the ball passing back and forth between his feet. He glanced up at the makeshift goal and launched himself forward, sweeping out his left leg and sending the ball flying past Andrea, between the orange cones, and straight through.

"Good," Andrea said as she retrieved the ball and set it on the ground in front of her. She kicked and sent it flying back to the other half of the field where it hit the side of the barn with a loud *thunk*. "One more time."

Andrew pushed his bangs off his forehead and wiped the sweat off with his hand. "You should be keeper for the girls' team," he said, deftly changing the subject, hoping to distract her from the practice and end it early.

"I don't like just standing there. I want to be running, you know that. No glory in standing still."

"You'd save the game," he pointed out, ambling back to the barn.

"I want to win the game, not save it. Besides, then we won't be the same position, you know?"

Andrew shrugged and picked up the ball. "It's not like we're on the same team anyway, so what's the difference? You're good at it."

Andrea flashed him an annoyed glare and picked up the cones. She didn't respond to him as they put the equipment away and shut off the floodlight. The field plunged into darkness and the two carefully made their way back to the house at the base of the hill.

Just as they reached the back door the alarm on Andrea's watch went off. She pressed the button, silencing it, and they crept inside. Upstairs they could hear movement from their parents' bedroom, and the coffeepot started to percolate on the kitchen counter.

Once in their shared room, Andrea nudged the door shut with her foot and flopped down on her bed face-first with a groan. "I'm so tired. I'm never doing that again," she said. Her voice came out muffled from the thick blankets.

Andrew knelt down and pulled out the bin under his bed, grabbing a pair of jeans and a long-sleeved polo. Yet again he bemoaned the fact that the renovations to his room still were not completed. *I really want my space back.* As he stood, the door swung open with too much force and hit the wall.

Their mother stood in the doorway, putting her earrings on, with a smile plastered to her face. "Breakfast will be ready soon. I'm making pancakes this morning."

Andrea ignored her and pulled the covers over her head while Andrew gathered his clothing. "I get the shower first."

"Take your time," Andrea grumbled from beneath the covers.

The bathroom stood just across the hall from the bedroom. Spread across the nearly nonexistent counter space was Andrea's makeup kit, which Andrew pushed aside as he set his things down. He grabbed a towel and got into the shower.

By the time he finished and had gotten dressed, Andrea was just getting up again. He went downstairs to the kitchen and heard the bathroom door slam behind him.

"Morning, Dad," Andrew said as he sat down in his chair and grabbed some pancakes off the steaming stack.

His father sat across from him, sipping a cup of coffee and reading the morning paper. "Morning," he said without looking up. "It's getting cold out. We're going to have to start the woodstove soon. Maybe later this week. We need more wood, though."

"Okay. I don't have practice after school tomorrow."

"All right. Tomorrow, then. Do you think one of your friends could come and help load up the woodshed?"

"I'll ask," Andrew said, and sipped his orange juice. He doubted any of them would volunteer, though. No doubt Andrea would find something to do, too.

"Did Andrea get up yet?" His mother stepped into the kitchen holding her purse. She set it down on the counter and lightly swatted her husband on the shoulder. "I told you a thousand times, no reading the paper at the table. You're going to get food all over it and I won't be able to read it later."

"She's in the shower. She'll be down in a few minutes," Andrew answered in response to his mother's question, ignoring the light admonition she gave to his father.

"Good. That girl's going to drive me crazy one of these days."

"Doesn't she already, dear?" His father didn't look up from his paper, but Andrew could see the hint of a grin on his face.

"Oh, shut up. You know what I mean."

Andrea came down to the kitchen a few minutes later, just as Andrew finished his breakfast. She poured herself a cup of coffee, which earned a glare from her mother.

"You better hurry and eat or you're going to be late. Coffee is not enough to keep you going until lunch."

"I'm not going to be late, Mom. Chill," Andrea said with a flippant wave of her hand. Andrew brought his dishes to the counter and set them there, pouring himself a small cup of coffee.

"Just eat your breakfast."

The rest of the short meal passed mostly in silence, with Andrew standing at the counter, warming his hands on the cup.

"Oh, Andrew. I need you to give these forms to Mrs. Conway in the office. They're for the school committee. She'll know which one."

"Okay," he said, setting the papers to the side.

Andrew grabbed Andrea's last piece of bacon and ran for the stairs before she could stab at him with a fork. He heard her frustrated yell all the way in the bathroom. A short time later he had brushed his teeth, fixed his hair, and was downstairs with his book and soccer bags. Andrea's things were already at the foot of the stairs. As an afterthought, he shoved his mother's papers in his book bag and zipped it shut.

"Bye, Mom. Bye, Dad," they both said as they ran for the truck.

"Drive carefully."

"Remember to hand those forms in for me, Andrew. They're due today."

It was cool outside, which did not surprise Andrew. He took a deep breath and let it out; he saw his breath in the air and a thin layer of frost covering the windshield of his old, gray pickup.

"Can I drive?" Andrea asked sweetly.

"No," he replied without hesitation, almost before she was able to finish her sentence.

It was the same routine every morning between the two of them. Andrew wouldn't let his sister drive his truck, and even though she asked every day, she never really pushed. They tossed their bags into the back, climbed into the truck, and slid across the cloth seats. To Andrew's immense relief, the truck turned over and started on the first try.

CHAPTER TWO

Cars and trucks only filled half of the student parking lot by the time the twins arrived at school. Andrew parked toward the back where most of the trucks were and they climbed out with their bags. Andrea waved to him and headed inside out of the cold, making a beeline toward a group of her friends. Andrew waved back and went straight to his locker.

After struggling with the combination lock for a few minutes and finally giving the locker a well-placed kick, it popped open and the contents shifted onto the floor.

Andrew stared at the pile and sighed before picking up the mess of papers. He shoved them back in the locker. *I should probably clean that at some point*, he thought. As he grabbed his math and history books, he heard a high-pitched shriek from close behind him, and he cringed.

"Andy! Hi! There you are. I've been looking all *over* for you this morning." Cynthia, varsity cheerleader and current girlfriend, came running over and threw her arms around him from behind. He fought a grimace and somehow managed a smile before turning to face her.

"Just got here."

"Oh, it's okay. I missed you. I'm sorry I had to cancel our plans last night. My parents had to go out of town, and like, they said I had to watch Justin. Little brat got sick," she said, making quotations in the air with her fingers.

"It's fine. I didn't mind. I hope he's feeling better."

"He's fine. But listen, you should come over tonight, okay? My parents are going to watch his tournament and won't be home."

Again, he fought another grimace. "I've got soccer practice after school, and then I made plans with Dad, sorry. Chores and all that, you know how it is. Can't get out of it."

"You're not even going to try?"

"Can't. He needs to get it done, and I already offered to help. I can't just back out on him."

"Oh…well, maybe later then…"

Andrew nodded and shouldered his bag. "Look, I gotta get to class. I'll see you at lunch."

Before she could protest, he took off in the direction of the office, relieved to get away. As he walked and waved at his classmates, he debated ending it with Cynthia. *It's been two months. That's gotta be long enough.* But how could he let her down without causing some sort of a scene? He snorted and shook his head. Breaking up with her was going to cause a scene no matter what. Cynthia loved drama. She lived for it. *I'll wait for the season to end. She'll be less distracting then.*

Andrew arrived at the office and opened the door. The room was pleasantly warm compared to the cooler hallways, and much quieter. Andrew approached the front desk and leaned over it. Next to him stood a boy he didn't recognize. After a cursory glance he ignored him and pulled out the forms his mother had given him.

"Hello, Andrew. What do you have there?" the secretary asked, a bright smile on her face.

"Some papers Mom wanted me to hand in. Forms or something."

"Oh, I know what they are. I'll take those, thank you."

"I'm finished with these, uh, Mrs. Conway," the boy next to Andrew said, leaning over the desk and letting the papers drop down in front of the secretary. His arm knocked into Andrew's as he did it, and Andrew knew it was on purpose. *What a jerk*, he thought as he pulled his arm out of the way and turned to leave.

"Sorry," the boy said, turning to face Andrew. He smiled and

Andrew stepped back, caught off guard by the intense green of his eyes.

"See you later, Mrs. Conway," Andrew finally said with a harsh intake of air.

"Bye, Andrew. Okay, Mr. Coltrane, here is your class schedule…"

Whatever else she said to the boy, Andrew didn't hear as the heavy office door slipped shut with a soft *schik* behind him. He navigated the halls by slipping between the crowds of students between the office and first-period history on the other side of the building.

So he's new here, Andrew thought as he walked. *Wonder where he's from.* The warning bell for first period interrupted his thoughts and he picked up his pace through the crowded, noisy hallway. Students loitered by their lockers and in doorways, greeting friends, laughing and joking. Someone was pushed against the lockers and an argument broke out, but a teacher stood nearby and broke it up. One small freshman fell into him as he passed by; Andrew caught him.

"Oh my gosh, I'm so sorry, Andy!" the smaller teen said.

"No worries." Andrew gave him a smile and shrugged before ducking into his classroom.

Mrs. Appleby was not there yet. He moved to the back of the room and the last row where he sat and dropped into his seat. He piled his books in front of him and opened his notebook. His friend Sarah was sprawled in the seat in front of him, her head down on the desk. Her breathing deepened, already asleep. Andrew reached over with a mischievous grin and nudged her shoulder. "Sarah, wake up."

She grunted in response and pushed at his hand.

"Come on, you can't be sleeping *before* class, you cheat."

"Andy," Sarah whined. She rubbed her eyes and sat up, stretching, and leaned back to rest her head on his desk. Her long, chocolate-colored hair pooled there. He flicked a strand off his book. "I had to study for Mr. Jackson's calc test last night. Do you know what time I finally managed to fall asleep?"

"No."

"Guess," she demanded.

"One?" Andrew raised an eyebrow.

"No! Try three. Three in the morning!" She groaned again and sat up, yawning. "I need coffee. No. You know what would be great? If they made caffeine an injection, like a drug? Yeah, I'd do it. Straight to the vein." She sighed heavily. "Sad thing is I'm still going to fail that test, even with all the studying. I hate calculus. What a waste of time."

Andrew laughed and shook his head as Mrs. Appleby walked in. "You're terrible."

"All right, class, let's settle down. Take your seats. Josh, get off your desk. We have a new student joining us today. Please be nice and welcome him, and none of the pranks you pulled last year, Michael," the teacher said, standing in front of her desk.

"Aww, Mrs. Appleby! No idea what you're talking about," Michael responded, and the class laughed.

"I'm sure you don't. Ryder, take a seat in the back next to Andrew."

Andrew looked up at the sound of his name and saw the student from the office walking down the aisle toward him. Sarah straightened up in her seat and giggled, then leaned to her right and started whispering to Karina, who leaned across the aisle to get her attention.

"This my seat?"

Andrew nodded. "No other one open."

"I'm Ryder Coltrane."

"Andrew Morris," he replied. He noticed a small accent, but he couldn't place it exactly. It sounded Southern, but which state, he couldn't tell. "Where you from?"

"Texas. Just moved up last week."

Andrew looked at him, curious. The sound of his voice enticed him, and he asked another question to hear more of it. "Texas? And you moved up here, to New York? Talk about a change. Must be a hell of a lot colder up here."

"Man, you have no idea. During winter in the South we don't

get anywhere near this cold. But it's all right." Ryder shrugged and opened his mouth when the teacher interrupted.

"Enough chatting. The two of you can get to know each other later. That goes for the rest of you, too. Stop gossiping. Josh, I told you before, get off your desk. Hand this book back to Ryder, please. Now, open up to page two hundred thirteen, and let's pick up where we left off. Ryder, see me after class and I'll give you copies of the notes for this chapter to catch you up." Mrs. Appleby moved behind her podium and opened her own book.

For the rest of the class, Andrew faded out. He followed along and spoke when he needed to, but he couldn't get into the lesson. Instead he focused on the guy sitting next to him. Even when sitting quietly, something about Ryder attracted attention. More than once Sarah turned around and looked at him, and then passed Karina a folded-up note. Andrew was tempted to lean over and snatch it out of their hands just to see what it said.

Ryder was tall, even when in his desk and slouched over. From standing next to him in the office Andrew guessed him to be six foot two, a good five inches taller than his own height. He had his hair cut longer than the style Andrew was used to seeing, and it fell to his chin in brown waves, just a shade or two lighter than Sarah's chocolate color. Ryder looked over at him at that moment and grinned. It was lopsided and…sort of cute, Andrew figured. *At least that's what Andrea would say.* And his eyes. A bright green that shone in the fluorescent lights. He noticed the color was unusual in the office, but now there was a light in his eyes that made them even brighter. He wore a dark green, long-sleeved shirt under a lighter green button-down, which only made his eyes stand out more.

Andrew jerked his head back to the front of the room and tried to focus on the teacher's words as his pulse raced. He frowned and tried to breathe, a little confused. *What's wrong with me? Am I coming down with something?* As he focused on his sudden condition, the bell rang.

"Remember, test on Friday for chapter seven. I expect an A from everyone!" Mrs. Appleby called as students began to file from the room.

"What class do you have next, Ryder?" Sarah asked, quickly crowding his desk with Karina and a few other girls.

"English with Mr. Ray."

"Oh, he's pretty cool, but I don't have him this year."

Andrew turned and walked up the aisle to leave.

"Hey, Andrew! Hold on a sec. What class do you have next?" Ryder pushed through the crowd around his desk and caught up with him.

"Study hall."

"Oh, damn."

Andrew shrugged. "See you at lunch, maybe."

Ryder grinned and tilted his head to the side. "Yeah, maybe."

❖

Andrew focused on the rest of his classes and made it all the way to lunch with barely any thought of Ryder. He met up with Andrea, Sarah, and Charlie, his friend from the soccer team. They got their lunches and sat at their usual table in the back corner of the cafeteria by the large windows that overlooked the school's courtyard. Andrew sat with his back to the room and poked at the mystery meat on his plate. The fork stuck and he removed it with an ominous sucking sound. He wrinkled his nose in disgust.

"So, Andrea, do you have any classes with Ryder?" Sarah asked as she poked her own mystery meat.

"Who?"

"The new guy," Sarah said with surprise. With a school as small as theirs, everyone knew when something big happened, usually within an hour of it occurring. And a new student definitely qualified as "a happening."

"No, guess not. No one new in my classes this morning," she responded.

"Oh, my God. You have to see him! He's so hot, isn't he, Andrew?"

Andrew rolled his eyes. "I don't know, Sarah. He's a guy."

"Right. You only do the cheerleaders. Then ditch them."

"Whatever."

"So what's going on with Cynthia?" Sarah asked, looking at him with wide eyes, clearly ready for gossip.

Andrew looked across the table at Charlie and suppressed a shudder. "She's getting annoying. This morning, she—"

"Ryder!" Sarah yelled and stood up, waving her arm. "Come sit here!"

"Ooh, he is pretty hot," Andrea agreed under her breath when he got closer. Andrew shook his head.

"Hey," Ryder said as he set his tray on the table and sat in the open seat next to Andrew.

"How's your first day, Ryder?" Sarah smiled flirtatiously, which he returned.

"It's going fine. I was pretty much at the same place y'all are in your classes back at my old school, so I'm not too far behind."

"That's cool. Hey, this is Andrea and Charlie."

Ryder nodded to them and then looked at Andrea, leaning across the table a bit. "You look familiar…are you in one of my classes?"

"No, but my brother is, apparently."

"Yeah? Who?"

Andrea laughed and nodded her head to Andrew. "Him."

Ryder turned and looked at him, then back to Andrea. And then back again. "Wait, you're twins? Wow. You look a lot alike." He stared at them both. Andrew knew what he was looking at: their identical dark blond hair and pale blue eyes. The only real difference between them, besides their gender, was the length of their hair; Andrew had his hair cropped short and spiked up with gel, and Andrea's hung just a little past her shoulders. Today she had pulled it back into a ponytail.

"We get that a lot," they answered in unison.

"Whoa, cool. Y'all do that twin speak thing often?"

"Twin what?"

"Twin speak. You know, talking at the same time, saying the same things. Can you, like, read each other's minds?"

Andrea stared at him. "No. We just spend so much time together, that's all. We used to be in the same classes together, too. But this year they split us up," she added with a small frown.

"Well, cool. I see where Andrew got his looks, then. He's real pretty like you, Andrea."

Everyone laughed, except for Andrew. His face turned a dark shade of red and he went back to poking at his lunch. "Ha ha. Funny."

"Aww, Andy. Don't get all upset. Don't mind him, Ryder. He just gets that. A lot," Charlie snickered, and he leaned back to avoid Andrew's hand as it reached across the table.

"We take after our mom. Andy's still a little touchy about that. Should have seen him when his hair was a little longer," Andrea said. "And when we were younger we were on the same soccer team. The coach mixed us up all the time."

"Yeah, they were nearly identical," Sarah agreed as she took a bite of her food. "I remember one time in third grade—"

"No!" Andrew lunged toward her and pressed a hand against her mouth, nearly falling over the table to do so. "He does *not* need to hear that story, okay?"

Ryder leaned forward. "What happened? You have to tell me now."

"Come on, don't, please," Andrew begged.

"Oh, just a little something." Andrea winked. Andrew felt her foot move past his leg while she kicked Sarah and Charlie under the table. "Maybe we'll tell you later."

"Damn, I want to know," Ryder said with lips turned down in a frown.

Andrew shook his head. "No. You don't."

"Yes, I do."

In an attempt to change the subject to something safer, especially in the presence of the new kid, Andrew said, "Hey, Charlie, Dad wanted to know if you could come help us load the woodshed. He's gonna start the stove and we could use some help."

Charlie eyed him suspiciously. "When?"

"Tomorrow after school since we don't have soccer practice."

"Gee, wish I could, but I got other plans."

Andrea rolled her eyes. "Sure you do."

"No really! I'm going shopping with Mom," he said, quickly occupying his mouth with his lunch.

"Hey, I could help. I've got nothing to do."

Andrew blinked a few times and looked at Ryder in disbelief. "We just met, and you're offering to help out?"

"Sure, why not? Like I said, nothing to really do around here. We could hang out after, maybe?"

"And get to be friends?" Andrea perked up, as did Sarah.

"I don't have many of those around here yet," he admitted. "It would be nice to replace those I lost from the move."

"Aren't you going to keep in touch with them? Isn't that what Facebook's for?" Charlie asked.

Ryder shrugged. "Facebook is one thing. But it's not like I could see them."

"Well, I think if you keep offering to help out with chores, you're gonna have people lined up to be friends," Andrea teased.

"Thanks for the offer, man," Andrew added.

"You can ride back with us after school tomorrow, right, Andy? I don't have practice either."

Andrew nodded and went back to his food before it became completely inedible. "Sure. I drive the old blue pickup parked in the back lot with the mismatched fenders. You can't miss it."

"So, what is it I'm not supposed to know?" Ryder stage whispered across the table. Andrew opened his mouth to protest and change the subject again.

"In third grade one of the boys in Andrew's class kissed him because he insisted Andrew was a girl!" Sarah laughed. Andrew's face grew hot, and he turned toward Ryder, ready to defend himself. Those green eyes stared back at him in amusement.

"Isn't that just cute," Ryder replied with a small wink at Andrew, and then went back to eating his food and asking questions about the school, town, and the twin's soccer teams.

Andrew waited for it to be brought up again, and then sighed with relief when it wasn't. *I could kill Sarah for telling him that*, he thought, mentally listing all the ways he could do it.

A loud crash interrupted his thoughts and made everyone at the table jump and turn toward the sound. At the opposite end of the cafeteria from where their table sat, a teen lay sprawled out on the floor. He pushed himself up on his elbows. From what Andrew could see, two other students stood over him, laughing.

"What's going on?" Ryder asked, frowning. He pushed himself up as if to go help, but Charlie reached out and grabbed his arm.

"That's Joshua Grayson. Don't worry about it. Not your problem."

"Why isn't it? Isn't someone going to help him?" he asked, even as the two other students walked away from him. The teen, Joshua, stood and dusted himself off, righted the chair that had been knocked over, and grabbed his tray. He left the cafeteria seconds later and the conversations around them resumed.

"It happens every so often," Sarah said with a shrug and continued eating.

"Why?"

"Josh is…you know," Charlie said, waving a hand limply.

"No, I don't know," Ryder said, but he sat back down.

"He's queer. A fairy."

Andrew looked up from his food. "Charlie, come on," he said sharply. The bell rang just then and Charlie stood.

"I'm just saying. Don't bother with him, Ryder."

Ryder and Andrew watched as Charlie walked away with Sarah and Andrea. Andrew stood after they disappeared into the body of students filing out into the hall.

"Why wouldn't anyone stand up for him?"

"Small town…small-town minds," Andrew replied with a shrug. "Come on. We'll be late for class."

CHAPTER THREE

When Andrew and Andrea came out of school the next afternoon, Ryder stood waiting by Andrew's truck, leaning up against the driver's side door. The weather had taken a turn for the worse and small flakes drifted down from the sky. A thin layer of snow covered the grass, but nothing stuck to the pavement yet; it just looked wet. The sound of students starting their cars and leaving felt distant, even though they were close by, and Andrew breathed in deeply, enjoying the crisp air.

"Damn, it's freezing!" Ryder complained, his arms crossed over his chest in a futile attempt to keep warm.

"What did you expect? This is upstate New York. You aren't in Texas anymore, cowboy," Andrea replied, her breath visible in the cold air.

"And it's so quiet, too. It's like I have cotton in my ears."

"The snow insulates the air. You should wait until there's a foot on the ground. A car can pass right in front of you and you won't hear it." Andrew unlocked the truck and they scrambled inside to get out of the cold with Andrea sitting in the center. It was not much warmer in the cab.

"And you're still going to play soccer in this mess?" Ryder asked once they were inside.

Andrew nodded. "This is nothing. It's an early snow. It won't last. The season will be over next week anyway. We're not going to state this year."

"No?"

Andrea shook her head. "Neither are the girls. Not enough seniors are playing, so half the team is new."

"And doesn't know how to play," Andrew added.

"That sucks."

This time Andrea nodded. "Yeah. I hoped we'd go one more time before graduation…but there's always college."

"You two are going to play in college?"

"If I get a scholarship I definitely am," Andrea said. "And if I get into a school with a good team I will. But I haven't decided where I'm going yet. It depends on what offers come up."

"I might, might not. It depends," Andrew said as he glanced around the lot and pulled out of his space.

"Of course you're playing in college," Andrea said, turning to look at him. Andrew glanced over and saw her eyes narrowed in determination.

Ryder, however, looked at them, impressed, as the truck joined the line of cars all trying to squeeze out of the narrow drive at the same time. Only the teacher's lot remained full. "Never knew anyone that went to college with a scholarship to play anything other than football."

They lapsed into silence once they finally pulled onto the main road and headed for home. Andrew took his time driving on the slick road.

"Where did you live in Texas?" Andrew finally asked, breaking the silence.

"About an hour south of San Antonio in a pretty small town. Well, small population wise. Nothing's small in Texas," Ryder said, chuckling. "Most of the town consists of large ranches. There used to be more people, but a lot moved into the cities."

"So your parents owned a ranch or something?"

"Nah, my dad was in the military and wanted to retire somewhere quiet. We moved around every three years when he had to change bases. It was annoying. But he retired there."

"What are you doing up here, then?" Andrea asked.

"He got recalled. He's stationed over in Germany now. Mom

went with him. They wanted me to finish high school here so they had me come up to stay with my aunt and uncle. They own a horse farm."

"The Kensingtons are your aunt and uncle?" Andrew asked, surprised. There was only one horse farm in town.

"Yeah, you know them?"

Andrea laughed. "Everyone knows everyone here. Of course we know them."

Once again, silence covered the truck as they bounced down one of the roads. Ryder kept his hand pressed against the door, making faces. The grimace faded when they pulled onto the next road and rounded the corner.

"Here we are," Andrew said, pulling into the driveway. His father's truck sat in the next spot over, the hood still warm and melting the snow that hit it.

"Nice. Really cozy."

"You have no idea," Andrea mumbled, and gave Andrew a shove to get him out of the truck.

The three teens piled out of the vehicle and Andrea sprinted into the house ahead of them. A wave of heat greeted them as they stepped inside and toed off their shoes. Inside the kitchen, their father poured himself a cup of coffee.

"Hey, Andy. Ready to get started on the wood? I figured we can get half of it filled today and the rest tomorrow." His father turned and sipped his coffee. He blinked when he saw Ryder standing next to Andrew. "Hello."

"Hi," Ryder said with a small wave of his fingers.

"Dad, this is Ryder. He just transferred here. He's Mr. and Mrs. Kensington's nephew."

"Oh yes, your uncle mentioned that you were coming up a couple of weeks ago. Have a good trip?"

"Yes sir," Ryder replied with a brief nod.

"Well, good to have you here. What happened to Charlie?" his father asked, directing his attention back to Andrew.

Andrew quirked his eyebrows and pressed his lips into a thin line. "He had to help his mother with shopping," he said, making air quotes.

"Right. The boy is lazy. Well then, I'll give you a few minutes to get ready. Then you can come around back, grab a pair of gloves, and we'll get started."

❖

Between Andrew, his father, and Ryder, they got more of the wood stacked than his father had planned. They decided to keep on working until they finished, even if it took them past dinner. The work went fast; Ryder was strong and could carry twice the amount of wood as Andrew, easily. *He's cutting down the load of work I would have had to do,* Andrew thought, eyeing his long, lean frame. It wasn't visible, but he had to work out. How else could he carry that much? Ryder turned and caught him staring and Andrew quickly ducked into the woodshed with the load he held.

In between loads, Andrew's father rested against the shed for a quick break. "So how's your mother doing?" he asked Ryder.

"You know my mother?"

"Of course! Rebecca, Kyle, Alice, and I went to high school together. Your uncle was a senior when we were freshman."

"That's so cool. I can't wait to tell Mom."

"Do you get to talk to her a lot?" Andrew asked.

Ryder shook his head. "Not on the phone. Calls to Germany can be expensive, so I don't call too much. We e-mail a lot, though, and Skype. She bought a new computer before she went over that has a built-in camera. She's doing well," he added. "She thinks Germany is great."

After unloading his last armful, Andrew's father dusted off his gloves and looked around. "That went fast. You're welcome to stay for dinner, Ryder. It's the least I could do to thank you," Andrew's father said, clapping a hand on his back. With that small movement, Andrew realized that even his father—whom he had considered tall before—stood shorter than Ryder.

"I'd love to, thank you." Ryder grinned, the smile lighting up his face.

"Now if only Charlie would be this useful," his father joked.

"That will never happen," Andrew replied.

❖

After dinner, the drive back to Ryder's place took less time than Andrew thought it would. He'd been out to the Kensingtons' farm a few times before, so he didn't need the directions Ryder attempted to give him. *Good thing*, he thought as he turned down a side road. *He has no clue where we are.* The snow had stopped falling and the roads were dry.

"Hey, thanks for helping me out today. You didn't have to do that," Andrew said as he pulled onto the long driveway leading to the farm. In the distance stood the large barn that housed the horses they boarded and bred.

"No big deal. Like I said, I had nothing to do. So," he added, "does this make us friends?"

Andrew laughed and parked the truck. "Maybe. If you come over every time I have to work."

"Cool."

Andrew waited for him to get out of the cab, but when he didn't, he glanced over at him. Ryder sat staring at him, silent. "What?"

Ryder shook his head and opened the door. "Come with me. I want to show you something."

"Nah, it's late. I've gotta get home."

"It'll just be a minute. Come on."

Shutting the door behind him, Ryder didn't give him much choice but to follow. Andrew scrambled to get out of the truck and catch up with him. His long legs made his stride lengthy.

Andrew followed him quietly to the horse barn where Ryder pushed the door open and flipped on a dim light. Inside, the sounds of horses moving about their stalls filled the air. In the first stall to their left, a horse came forward into the light and nickered softly at the sight of them. Ryder's eyes warmed and he made his way over to the stall, pausing for a moment to grab a box from the shelf beside it.

"Hey, Cobalt. Miss me?" he asked gently while he rubbed between the horse's eyes. He pushed his other palm up to its mouth. The horse lipped up the small, white cube and munched on it. The ears pricked forward as he looked toward Andrew.

"This is my horse, Cobalt," Ryder said when Andrew didn't move from inside the doorway. "Brought him up from Texas with me. Couldn't deal with leaving him behind or selling him. Aunt Lisa and Uncle Kyle said they had some free space."

"I thought you said you didn't live on a ranch."

"We didn't. Doesn't mean I can't have a horse. I boarded him at the Moorhead Ranch. Worked there after school mucking out stalls to pay for it. You ever been riding?"

"Do pony rides at the county fair count?" Andrew asked sheepishly.

Ryder laughed and shook his head. "Nah, those don't count. You should come over one time. I'll take you riding for real."

"I'd probably fall off."

"And you live in the countryside?"

"I never claimed to be a farmer."

Ryder looked at him and Andrew felt like he was being inspected. He shifted uneasily after a few moments of silence. "No, I guess you didn't," Ryder finally said. He turned back to Cobalt and scratched behind an ear. Even though his eyes were no longer on him, Andrew still felt like squirming.

"Do you do a lot of work around here?"

"Yeah. I don't mind, though. Not since they let me bring Cobalt up. Same stuff I did back home: mucking out stalls, feeding, watering. Giving them exercise." He looked over at Andrew, eyes bright with excitement. "I can't wait to go riding in the snow."

"What's so special about that?" Andrew stepped closer and put his hand out to let the horse sniff it.

"Oh come on! Think about it. Nothing but a white landscape all around you, sparkling in the sun. Or at night. In the moonlight."

"Wow, you sound like someone out of a romance novel," Andrew teased. "You'll get along great with Andrea and Sarah."

Ryder shrugged and eyed him. "Maybe I am romantic."

Andrew waited a few moments before saying, "Hey, I have a soccer game next Saturday. It's at the school. You should come to it."

"I don't really know much about the sport, though," Ryder said, tilting his head to the side.

"That's fine. It's the last game before the season ends."

"Maybe I'll go just to watch you," Ryder said. His eyes were intense and darker in the dim light of the barn. Andrew suppressed a shiver and crossed his arms over his chest when his heart skipped a beat. *I'm definitely catching something. I better not get too sick before the game or Coach will kill me.*

"That's cool. We need all the support we can get. It's going to be a good game. The last one is always the most exciting. And there's nothing to lose."

"You said earlier you weren't going to go to the finals, though, right?"

"Yeah. The team we're playing against is tough. They're our rival school over in Hanson. Last year we beat them and went to finals, but their record is much better than ours this year. But we'll still try like hell." He paused before adding, "I won't make winning easy for them."

Ryder leaned up against the stall door. "I'm sure you won't."

CHAPTER FOUR

Saturday came and Andrew woke up early to get ready for the game. It was scheduled to start at ten, but he had to be there by eight for warm-ups. He looked out the window over Andrea's bed as he grabbed his track pants and saw that the sky had cleared and no trace remained of the little snow that had been left the night before on the ground. It was a beautiful day to play.

He showered quickly and dressed, then joined his parents downstairs.

"The paper is saying Hanson's the favorite to win," his father said from behind the paper. Andrew shrugged and tied the laces of his sneakers.

"Maybe so, but we'll give them hell."

"I wish we had a shot at going to state," Andrea complained while pulling her hair up into a ponytail. "But they already beat us this year and the girls' record is flawless; we've lost seven games. We lost too many seniors at the end of last season. It sucks."

"Plus some of the girls didn't come back to play this year, either," Andrew said.

"And Megan had to quit halfway through because of her grades."

"See why I keep on you about your homework?" their mother asked from the other room. "If I didn't, you'd be in the same situation."

Andrea just rolled her eyes and nudged her brother. The two

of them got up to collect the rest of their gear. "We've gotta leave soon, Dad."

"That's fine. Your mother and I will meet you at the school before the game starts. Yours is at two, right, Andrea?"

"Right."

Andrew started the truck ten minutes later and headed for the school grounds.

"The other day when you were talking to Ryder, were you serious about not playing soccer in college?" Andrea asked, leaning back against the door of the truck so that she could face him.

"I've thought about it," he replied hesitantly.

"Andy, we always said we'd play straight through!"

Andrew pressed his lips in a tight line and took a moment to answer. "I know. I just said I thought about it. It doesn't mean I won't."

"You have to play. We have plans. You can't just go change them without talking to me about it first," she argued.

"I'm sorry, okay? The next time something big comes up I'll talk to you about it."

"I hope so," she murmured. "You never kept anything from me before. We're still picking a school together, right? Or did you change your mind about that, too?"

Andrew nodded. "Of course not. We pick together."

Only a few cars were in the parking lot when they arrived, and Andrew parked next to Charlie, who waited for them in his car.

"Great day to play!" Charlie called as they all climbed out. "It's so warm compared to last week. Thank God."

"Yeah, right? We lucked out," Andrea agreed.

Members of the team were already gathering down at the field and stretching out. Andrea parted from them to join the girls, most of whom came early to support the boys' team.

Andrew and Charlie found an open spot and helped each other warm up. Andrew sat on the ground and leaned forward, and Charlie pushed against his back, then they switched positions. Their coach showed up a short time later, and soon after, the other team arrived at the field to do their own warm-ups.

Parents and students arrived half an hour before the game. There were two sets of bleachers on one side of the field, and they quickly filled. Andrew turned to see his parents in the top row. Charlie's parents sat right below them and a few seats over Andrew saw another familiar face. He waved at Ryder, who saw him and waved back. The coach called the team into a huddle, and Andrew jogged over to join the group.

"This is it, guys," Coach Matthews said, his face trying to look serious but barely managing it. "Last game of the season. Hanson is going to be tough, but let's show them we won't go down without a fight. We can do this, right?"

The team yelled their agreement and cheered.

"All right, let's show them what we're made of! Keep your focus and go for it! Keep control of the ball and keep it on their side of the field. Don't give them the opportunity to take a shot at our goal. Nielsen, focus on that ball and do not let it pass you."

The keeper nodded. "Got it, Coach."

The referee called Pete Williams, the captain of Andrew's team, forward with Hanson's captain. The two stood facing each other while the man tossed the coin and let it fall to the ground. He called out and gestured to the other side of the field as Pete jogged back to them.

"Hanson won the kickoff."

Coach Matthews nodded. "All right, let's get out there and play!"

The teams met on the field and everyone took their places at least ten yards back from the center circle where the ball would be kicked. From his place on the field, Andrew glanced up quickly, surprised to see his dad and Ryder sitting together. He turned his attention back to the game, narrowing his focus to the opposition and his teammates.

Hanson's forward charged the ball and let it sail with a solid kick. Andrew turned to watch as Charlie jumped up; the ball collided with his chest and dropped to the ground, where he sent it flying in Andrew's direction.

Andrew took possession of the ball and dribbled down the field, focused on the goal at the other end, but aware of his teammates moving up the field with him. He heard someone yell, "Andy! Man on!" from behind him, and quickly passed the ball to Pete.

The captain feinted to the left when an opponent ran at him, but the play failed. The player with Hanson's maroon and white jersey slid on the ground and kicked the ball away from Pete. His teammate just behind him took possession of the ball and they raced back for the other side of the field.

Andrew did his best not to swear in frustration and ran after them to avoid being called offside. As the ball reached their goal, Nielsen stepped forward and saved it, scooping the ball with his hands and sending it flying back to the other side of the field.

Nice save, Andrew thought, giving a thumbs-up to the keeper as he ran back down the other side of the field.

The first twenty minutes of the first half passed without a single score. Andrew was switched off the field, and he sat and drank some water while watching his teammates play. He cheered them on and yelled whenever Hanson took the ball. The other team scored the first goal, and by the end of the first half, the score stood at 1–0.

Andrew got off the bench and moved into the huddle with his team during the fifteen-minute break between halves, but movement caught his attention. He turned as his coach started talking about strategy and saw Ryder waving. He grinned and gave him a small wave, and then stopped.

What am I doing? I need to be focused on Coach, not waving at Ryder like an idiot.

He turned back to listen and tried to keep his thoughts on the game and far from the green-eyed Texan sitting in the stands. Why he entered his thoughts at a time like this Andrew had no idea.

The second period flew by, and Andrew was put on the field again in the last fifteen minutes. He quickly scored a goal by dragging his right foot across and cutting back with his left. The move got him past the other side's defense and he took the shot. The ball sailed right into the open net, and he ran back to his cheering teammates. The score remained tied until the last five minutes, when one of Hanson's forwards snuck the ball past Nielsen and scored a goal. Andrew and his teammate Michael tried to even the score and raced across the field, but the clock ran down before they could make it and the game ended.

Loud cheers came from Hanson's side, and disappointment crushed Andrew. *So damn close.* The way the game had been going, he had been sure they were going to win. He joined the rest of the team on the field to shake hands with their rivals. Coach Matthews was as deflated as they were, but he congratulated the team on playing a great game.

"It has been a privilege to work with you this year. Seniors, this may have been your last year, but you gave it your best. I'm proud to have worked with you. For those of you playing in college, I better get invitations to some of your games!"

They laughed and slowly parted ways. Ryder came down from the stands and walked toward Andrew.

"That goal you made was amazing!"

"Not really," Andrew said, shrugging. "The goalie screwed up; he left the net wide open. I had a free shot."

"You're being modest," Andrea said from behind him, a second before she jumped on his back. "You totally nailed that shot and you know it. Our early-morning practice really paid off." She held on tight and Andrew reached back to support her weight and keep from being strangled. "Did you see who was watching the game?" she squealed with excitement in his ear.

"Kind of hard to do that when I was playing, Andy."

"There were scouts! I'm sure of it! I think there were four or five of them sitting in the stands. They were watching you!"

"Oh come on. Are you sure they were scouts?"

"Who else wears suits to a soccer game?"

"Parents just getting out of work?" he asked.

She flicked his ear and slid off his back. "On a Saturday morning? You're more of an idiot than I thought."

"Fine, but I'm sure they were looking at Hanson's captain. Or Pete."

"Again with the modesty. Cut the crap. They were watching you. Just wait. You'll have offers. We both will. Hey, Ryder," she called as she jogged backward to her teammates. "Are you sticking around to watch my game? Andrew always does, for support."

Ryder glanced at Andrew. "I don't see why not. Your father got me caught up with the terms and such. Are you a forward too, Andrea?"

She nodded. "Yup. But I play midfield too, like Charlie, if one of the girls is out."

"That's pretty cool."

"She could also play as the keeper; she's good enough."

"But—"

"But," Andrew glanced at Ryder and cut off her protest. "But she likes taking the glory, and you don't get that from standing there and saving shots."

Andrew joined his parent in the bleachers. Ryder moved up and sat with them, apologizing to those around him as he squeezed in close to Andrew.

Throughout the girls' game, the boys cheered them on while Andrew told Ryder more about the game, and pointed out the different students. The final score was 3–1, with Andrea having missed her shot. She stalked off the field, anger pouring off her in waves.

On the ride home, Andrea fumed, which both Ryder and Andrew had to endure. She sat between them and every so often let out a frustrated growl low in her throat. Andrew watched Ryder try to keep from bursting out with a laugh, but he finally couldn't help himself.

"Don't laugh!" Andrea said.

"I'm sorry! You sound so funny!" He dodged her flying hand, but he could only get so far from her reach. Andrew wisely kept a laugh to himself and concentrated on driving.

"I missed an easy shot! That is not funny!"

"Well, you would have lost the game anyway, right?"

"That's not the point! They beat us by two whole points! It would have been a lot closer if mine had gone in," Andrea argued.

"But," Ryder replied, "if you had gotten yours in, you would have been pissed that you only missed by one point. Right?"

Andrea grudgingly agreed that he was right, but either way the game had still been a loss. *I'm going to have to deal with this attitude all day*, Andrew thought as he turned onto their road. *If she keeps me up all night complaining I'll dump her makeup in the trash.*

CHAPTER FIVE

The soccer season had ended just as Andrew suspected it would; they didn't make it to the state level. Andrea's guess about the scouts had been right, though, which the coach confirmed the following Monday morning when he called Andrew into his office to talk about it.

Despite the scouts, Andrew tried not to get his hopes up. *We're not going to get a scholarship*, Andrew thought as he left the locker room. Coach Matthews had told him not to give up, but it didn't matter. *Those promises never hold up.* There were no more games. What were the scouts supposed to watch? Andrea would be pissed, though. She'd be impossible to live with if they didn't get an offer.

The first real snowfall came the following day. The snow was heavy and left seven inches on the ground overnight, leaving a mess all over the roads. On the way to school, Andrew now made it a point to swing by the Kensingtons' place to pick up Ryder, who much preferred the cold truck cab to the cold bus.

That particular morning Andrea had woken up with a sore throat and no voice, and begged, silently, to stay home. Their mother agreed to it and ordered her to stay in bed, which meant Andrew would have a quiet ride out to Ryder's place without Andrea harassing him about college.

"Where's Andrea?" Ryder asked as he slid across bench seat, dumping his bag on the floor.

"Home sick. Sore throat."

"Think she's faking it?"

"No, it's real. She looked like crap. She even wanted me to stay home and take care of her." He laughed.

"Ah."

Even with Ryder in the cab it was quiet but not uncomfortable. Ryder fiddled with the radio for a few minutes before giving up. "Radio sucks."

"It's the snow interfering with the signal. Or something."

"No, your radio just sucks."

They grinned at each other from across the bench seat. Few cars filled the school parking lot when they pulled in. "I bet a lot of kids skip today," Andrew said as he threw the truck in park and they climbed out.

"Do you ever get like, snow days up here?"

"Yeah, when it's really bad."

"What do you consider really bad?"

"Um, when the roads are covered in ice. Or when there's more than a foot of fresh snow on the roads. Blizzard. Nor'easter. Things like that."

"Think we'll have one soon?"

"I don't know, maybe. Hard to tell at this point." Andrew waited a moment before he added, "It was a quiet ride without Andrea. I liked it."

Ryder glanced over at him, one eyebrow quirked. "Oh? I thought you two were inseparable," he joked.

"Yeah, well, it's nice to have space sometimes."

Andrew walked into the school with Ryder close behind him and the two stomped the snow off their shoes. Just past the doormat someone had placed a yellow caution sign, warning anyone who entered of water on the floor. The boys headed for their lockers.

Cynthia stood at hers when they walked past, and she slammed the door shut and walked away, nose in the air.

"What was *that* all about?" Ryder asked, turning to watch her leave.

"I broke up with her," Andrew replied calmly.

"When?"

"After the season ended. The day after, I think."

"Why didn't you tell me?"

"Why, you interested?" Andrew glanced at him.

Ryder laughed and stared at him. "You think I would be interested in her? That's funny."

"Well, whatever. She's not seeing anyone if you wanted to ask her out. At least she wasn't yesterday, who really knows now."

"Nah, I'm interested in someone else," Ryder said as he fiddled with the combination on the locker he leaned against.

The words shocked Andrew and he looked up at him. *He likes someone already? He just moved here.* Curiosity got the best of him and he asked, "Really? Who?"

Ryder just shrugged noncommittally and moved to his locker a few spaces down.

Andrew wanted to press him further, but Danielle Fisher walked past Ryder and wormed her way between him and Andrew. "I thought you were going to call me last night."

Andrew swore under his breath, looking sheepish. "I'm sorry, Danielle. I totally forgot."

"You forgot? You forget a lot, Andy. At least that's what I hear. Are we still on for tonight?"

"Yeah, sure. Of course." Andrew leaned forward and quickly kissed her. Danielle wrapped her arms around his neck and pulled him down against her, not letting him pull back. After long seconds, she let go, blew him a kiss, and took off down the hall.

This one isn't going to last two months, Andrew thought as he stared into his locker.

"Okay, you didn't tell me about Cynthia, and I know you didn't tell me about Danielle. When the hell did that happen?"

"Must have slipped my mind. She got to me right after I broke up with Cynthia. I didn't think it was that big a deal." Andrew felt uncomfortable with the conversation and shoved books into his locker.

"Dating someone slipped your mind? Andy, do you *like* girls?"

"What? Of course! Why would you say that?" He looked up at Ryder, horrified.

"Because every time I see your girlfriend, or whatever you'd call Danielle, touch you? You get this look on your face."

"A look?"

"Yeah, like you're sick," Ryder replied seriously.

Andrew choked and shook his head. "No, I like it. They just get clingy after a while. Can't stand that."

"Right…"

"What?" Andrew frowned, slamming the locker shut. He didn't like the tone of Ryder's voice.

"Nothing," his friend said and turned away from him.

"Well, it's not really any of your business anyway, who I date or don't."

"I thought we were friends."

"We are."

Ryder tilted his head and looked back at him with a strange look on his face. Andrew couldn't describe it, but he thought for a moment that Ryder could see right inside him. "Isn't that something you tell your friends about? Or are things different up here? Because down in Texas, the guys bragged about it all the time whenever they scored a hot one. And last I checked, Danielle would fit that description."

Confused by his own anger, Andrew grabbed his things, taking off for first period. Ryder followed behind him seconds later, matching his stride with his long legs.

"Andrew, wait—"

He spun to face Ryder. "Okay, look. Maybe dating is not something I really care about so much, but I have a—"

"If you say a reputation to protect, I'll punch you right now."

"What?" Andrew stopped, startled. Why would that deserve a punch? And could Ryder even do that? His lips turned down in a small frown. No, definitely not. Ryder didn't seem capable of hurting a fly. Andrew had never even heard Ryder raise his voice.

"What kind of reputation would you have to protect? Everyone in this school thinks you're awesome. I'm new and I know that already. The girls love you. The guys want to be you," he said as a sly grin crossed over his face. "Hell, some of the guys want you, too."

Andrew felt the heat creep into his face, sure it had turned a shade that bordered on fire engine red. Without replying, he headed toward class in a brisk walk.

"You don't have to protect anything," Ryder pressed, catching up with him again. "No one would care. Why should they? You're a cool guy to hang with."

"Maybe."

"Maybe nothing," Ryder argued.

"I've dated a lot of girls. It's kind of expected by now, I guess."

"Man, that is bullshit."

Andrew did a double take. "Is that why you don't date? Because you think it's bullshit? Sarah wants you, you know." Andrew shifted his books to the other arm and opened the door to their history class.

"Yeah, I know, but I don't want her." Ryder stopped him from entering the classroom with a light grip on his wrist. "She's not my type."

"What is your type?" Andrew asked, genuinely curious. He let the door shut, muffling the sounds of their classmates.

"Not that."

"Just 'not that'?"

"Yup," Ryder grinned.

Andrew sighed and shook his head. "You can be so cryptic."

"Your life was boring before I got here, being all cryptic. Admit it. I bring excitement."

Andrew regarded him thoughtfully and seriously for a moment before grabbing the door handle again. "You bring something, all right. I just don't know what."

❖

Class that morning consisted of a pop quiz that they were informed came from a test they had the next week. The entire class groaned in unison at the thought of yet another test. While they were reviewing, Ryder leaned across the aisle toward Andrew, speaking softly and keeping his face on the front of the classroom to watch for Mrs. Appleby. The teacher stood with her back to the room, pointing out various battle locations on a map, occasionally consulting her textbook.

"Hey," he said, his voice a near inaudible murmur, but Sarah turned to look at him curiously. He waved a hand and she pouted but turned to face the front again. Ryder dropped his voice even lower.

"What? You're going to get us in trouble," Andrew muttered.

"You should come over and ride tonight."

"I told you, I don't know how to ride."

Ryder quirked the corner of his lips up and leaned closer. "So you've said. But I'll teach you. It's not so hard. We have a lot of calm horses," he added. When Andrew hesitated, he nudged him gently. "Come on. What do you say?"

"All right…I'll call Danielle and tell her I can't come over," he said, feeling a bit relieved by the new plans and guilty at the same time. But the relief outweighed the guilt. Karina glanced back at him, her eyes questioning, and he shook his head.

He'd just tell Danielle something came up with Andrea.

She'd have to understand.

CHAPTER SIX

"S he dumped you for changing your plans? Man, that's harsh," Ryder said as they pulled up to his house.

She had been upset, but okay with changing the date until Andrew had slipped up and mentioned that it was Ryder's house he was going to, not home to take care of Andrea. And that's when she lost it. "I guess I deserved it, though. I promised her, and then I broke the promise to hang out with you," Andrew lamented. "But worse, I lied about it at first."

"You lied? Fatal mistake."

"I guess." He parked the truck and sat there with his hand draped over the steering wheel, staring out the window. "Girls can be so...I don't know—"

"Annoying? Frustrating? Fickle? Conceited? Confusing? All of the above?" Ryder started, ticking off descriptions on his fingers. Andrew glanced at him and rolled his eyes. At least one of them appeared to be having fun with this. Andrew continued to brood, taking in the Kensingtons' farm. The lights were on in the barn, and in the house the kitchen light shone brightly through the curtains. From the chimney a light plume of smoke rose over the buildings.

"Why are you so broken up over it? It didn't seem like you really liked her that much."

"I didn't. But"—Andrew felt sheepish—"I haven't gotten laid in weeks."

Ryder shook his head and climbed out of the vehicle. "Oh, poor you. Come on."

The snow from the last storm crunched lightly underfoot as they walked to the barn. Dumping their bags on a table in the corner, they walked down the row of stalls to find Kyle Kensington mucking out one of them. He didn't notice them for a minute and continued to work in silence.

"Hey, Uncle Kyle," Ryder said. The man started and whipped around, breathing a sigh of relief.

"Ryder! You scared me, son. Don't sneak up on me like that."

"Sorry, but we weren't really *that* quiet."

"No matter. Hello, Andrew."

"Hi, Mr. Kensington."

"I brought Andrew over to ride. He's never been before," Ryder said, walking to one of the stalls and scratching the cheek of the horse inside.

"All right. Be careful. And take Magpie. She hasn't been exercised yet." Finishing up with the stall, Ryder's uncle put some new hay down and disappeared with the wheelbarrow out the door.

Magpie was a black-and-white mare. Her head and back were a dark, nearly blue black, and her chest, shoulder and barrel were a snowy white. She greeted them at the door of her stall and leaned over, lipping Ryder's palm for a nonexistent treat. Ryder chuckled softly.

"Sorry, Magpie. I don't have anything just yet. Andy, this is Magpie. Magpie, Andy."

Andrew felt a little foolish talking to the horse. But Ryder was doing it, so what the heck? "Uh, hello."

"It's okay to talk to a horse. They can understand you. I talk to Cobalt all the time," he added for reassurance. Andrew nodded. "All right, let's get you set up." Grabbing the lead rope tacked up outside the stall, Ryder clipped it onto her halter, opened the door, and led her out.

"Don't I need something to sit on?" Andrew asked, looking at the horse skeptically. Ryder laughed at him as he tied the mare up to ropes between the stalls. "What's that for?"

"We'll get you a saddle in a second. This is to keep her in place while we get her ready. After we ride, we'll groom them. But right now, before we go, I like to give the horses a quick brush before I put the saddle on, and then I check the hooves."

"Oh, but…" Andrew indicated the ropes.

"If we don't tie them up on both sides and you're working here," Ryder said as he stood between the horse and one wall, "the horse can lean against you and push you into the wall. Especially if you're giving them a good brushing. They like that. But I guarantee you wouldn't."

Andrew nodded and followed him as he got Cobalt out of his stall and led him to a space a few feet behind Magpie and tied him up as well. Then he motioned for Andrew to follow him through a door at the other end of the barn from the one they entered.

"Where are we going? Is it okay to leave them like that?"

"It's fine," Ryder said, flipping on the light. "This is the tack room. We keep all the hardware we need to ride in here. Saddles, saddle pads, harnesses, halters, bridles, you name it. It's all here."

"You just spoke Greek, because I have no idea what you said." Andrew looked around the small room and noted all the cubbies with various leather contraptions in them or hanging next to them. Saddles filled half of the boxes, with long, leather ropes next to each. He gingerly reached out and touched one.

Ryder watched him, amused. Looking over the saddles, he found Magpie's and frowned, glancing from the saddles, to Andrew, and back again.

"What is it?"

"I'm just debating whether to put you in an English saddle or Western for your first time."

"What's the difference?" Andrew asked, looking over the two saddles. He could visibly see the difference as soon as he got a look at them. "Oh."

"Yeah. The English saddle has no horn to hold on to. It's smaller, lightweight, better padded. The stirrups are a little smaller… stirrups!"

Confused by the sudden change in tone, Andrew turned to look at him and blinked. "What about the stirrups?"

"You're wearing sneakers. You need boots. It's easier to keep your foot in the stirrup when you have a heel so you don't slip through. What size shoe are you?"

"Ten," he answered, still mystified.

"I think my uncle is a size ten, hold on." Ryder disappeared through a door Andrew hadn't noticed at the back of the tack room. Inside, the lights flipped on for a moment and then back off. Ryder emerged holding a pair of worn, brown boots in his hand. "Yeah, these should fit you. I'll just let him know you borrowed them. He shouldn't mind."

"Um…what were you saying before about the saddles?"

"Oh! Right. The stirrups are smaller than a Western style," which he gestured toward. "They use these at the fairs for those pony rides you take."

"Took, Ryder. Took." Andrew felt his face heat again.

Ryder rested his hands on his hips and leaned against the wall. "Fine, took. They're heavier with sturdier stirrups, and they have the horn. I guess it is okay to use when you first learn because you can hold on to it, but it's not as comfortable. I use an English saddle. I think you should too this time, and we'll see what you think."

"Don't cowboys use those? The Westerns?"

"Well, yeah. So?"

"So…you lived in Texas."

"That doesn't make me a cowboy, Andy."

Grabbing a saddle and saddle pad, Ryder dumped them in Andrew's arms and then grabbed one of the rope-like contraptions Andrew had noticed and settled that over the saddle. "That's the bridle," Ryder explained as he debated the helmets.

"I'm not wearing a helmet."

"You're new, you're wearing one. Don't argue."

The tone in his voice wouldn't allow for any argument. It was firm and very businesslike. Ryder was a different person outside of school. Andrew liked it. "What about you?"

"What about me?" Ryder asked.

"Aren't you going to wear a helmet?"

"I've been riding for years. I can manage without one if we're just in the field."

Andrew glared as Ryder fitted the helmet to his head, then satisfied with the size, plopped it onto the stack Andrew already held. Andrew watched his friend pick up the same equipment for himself—minus a helmet. Ryder carried his stuff gracefully out of the room. Andrew followed behind, struggling a bit under the cumbersome weight and nearly tripping over a rope that rested on the floor in his direct path.

"I'll put Cobalt's things on first, and you can watch, and then we'll work on Magpie together."

Setting the things down on a bench as directed, Andrew traded his sneakers for the boots. They stowed their shoes under the bench seat outside Cobalt's stall. Before they got started, Ryder showed him how to check the hooves for any debris and clean them out, and then gave Cobalt a quick brush over his back. When he put on the saddle pad and saddle, he moved quickly and Andrew could not keep up with the swift pace. He stared at the bridle as Ryder slipped it over Cobalt's head, over the halter, and made a face.

"What?" Ryder asked when he glanced back over his shoulder.

"I'm lost."

"Don't worry. I'll help you." Leaving the halter tied to the crossties for the moment, they worked on the mare next. The two had to work close in the narrow space between the horse's body and the walls, and soon they were getting in each other's way as Ryder guided Andrew's hands. When their bodies brushed together for the fifth time, not that Andrew was counting, he felt an uncomfortable flush start on his cheeks and silently prayed it wouldn't spread to his neck. The air grew thick with tension as they prepared the horse. Ryder brushed up against him again, and Andrew shivered despite the heat from the horse's body.

"You cold?" Ryder asked.

"Uh…a little."

Not seeming to notice Andrew's discomfort, Ryder stepped back. "You'll warm up."

"I'm sure I will."

"All right." Ryder added, "Helmet on. We're ready."

Andrew put the helmet on with a scowl and left it unbuckled. Ryder unclipped the crossties and showed him how to slide the halter off from underneath the bridle, and then they were off, walking side by side with the horses following.

"We'll head out to the west field. It's flatter."

"Whatever you say," Andrew said.

Once they passed through the fence and locked it in place behind them, Ryder helped Andrew climb up on the horse. Standing on the left side, he pulled the stirrup down and showed him how to put his foot in and pull himself up.

"It's easier with a horn," he admitted. "And we have to adjust the stirrups for your leg length." After another few awkward moments with Ryder's hands tugging his legs this way and that to get the length just right, he was settled. Ryder climbed up on Cobalt and Andrew followed him at a walk through the field.

Andrew soon became comfortable with riding because of the slow gait of the horse. Magpie could be controlled with just the slightest, gentle guiding of the reins and Andrew turned her where he wanted to go. He tested out his power over the large animal by gently tugging first to the left, then the right. Magpie's ears flicked back at him and she snorted. Ryder pulled up next to him with Cobalt and their legs nearly brushed together.

"Not so bad, huh?"

"Yeah, it's not bad," Andrew admitted.

"Make sure you use your legs to stay on. You should use your thighs to grip the horse. Don't rely on the reins to keep you in the saddle. You could drop them right now and stay on," Ryder said and dropped his to demonstrate. Cobalt kept walking in the same direction.

"No thanks," Andrew said, unsure. He had no desire to look like a fool today.

"Just don't put too much weight on the stirrups. It'll make you unsteady."

Andrew watched him, a little skeptical, but agreed to do his best. They walked around the field at a slow, easy pace. Andrew relaxed and let his thoughts wander to the calm, early winter evening. The sun moved closer to the horizon as they rode, casting a calming light over everything.

When they were about midway through the field, Cobalt broke into a run and Andrew gently pulled Magpie back with the reins to watch Ryder and his horse make a circuit of the field. When his friend joined them again, he was laughing and patting the horse's neck. His cheeks were flushed from the wind and his hair fell in messy strands around his face.

"That was amazing," Andrew admitted, staring at him with wide eyes.

"You'll learn. We'll go slowly. Cobalt knows me, and I know him. That's important."

"You make it look so easy."

"It is, really. Once you've done it a few times it's not bad." Pulling back lightly on the reins, Ryder stopped, and Andrew stopped next to him. "I think we'll stop for today. Don't want you to get sore in the saddle."

"I'm fine, really," Andrew insisted.

"Trust me. It feels okay now, but after you've ridden for a few hours, you won't be saying that. Let's head back to the barn. I'll show you how to groom Magpie."

The pair took the ride back to the barn just as slow and easygoing as the one out to the field. They joked about different things: school, girls, and their friends. A few times Ryder would bring Cobalt close and their legs would press together between the horses. Andrew felt that same strange heat from before fill him. He looked around, sheepishly, sure his face was red. He hoped he'd be able to pass it off as an effect from the cold air.

"You feeling okay?" Ryder asked after a few minutes of silence. Andrew simply nodded.

Riding out here like this with Ryder...it felt good. He couldn't do something like this with Charlie. And Andrea would never go for it. It wasn't enough excitement for her.

Andrew was about to voice these thoughts when they spotted someone waving and running toward them along the fence. It was Ryder's uncle. He shouted and gestured toward the other field, separated from the one they were in by a low fence made out of short posts and bars. Inside that field a horse ran with its lead rope dangling from the halter. They could just make out his uncle's shouts as they drew closer.

"Dante broke lose again!"

Ryder groaned. "Stay here," he instructed.

"What are you doing?"

"Going to get the damn horse back. Come on, Cobalt."

Andrew watched as horse and rider wheeled in a tight circle and Cobalt took off straight for the fence. As they approached it, Andrew realized they were going to run right into it if they didn't turn or slow down. *He's going to kill himself!* He wanted to call out to Ryder to be careful but knew the wind would suck his words away unheard. He cringed, wondering what the damage would be, and watched in amazement when the pair effortlessly jumped the fence, landed on the other side, and kept going. Andrew couldn't believe they'd made that jump! Heart racing, he pressed a hand against his chest. Ryder's uncle wheezed when he reached Andrew, struggling to catch his breath.

"That boy is a daredevil, I'll tell you. Him and that horse. They make a great pair, though, wouldn't you say?"

"Yeah," Andrew agreed, in awe. He kept his gaze on Ryder and watched as he and his horse caught up with the one loose. Ryder reached out, stretching his long body over Cobalt's neck, and grabbed hold of the other horse's lead. "He makes it look so easy."

"He's been riding since he was a boy, and he's had that horse for I think close to five, six years now. I couldn't say no when he wanted to bring him along. I know what it's like to have to get rid of a horse. It's not fun." A beat passed. "How's old Magpie treating you?"

"Huh? Oh, she's great," Andrew answered, distracted by the loose-limbed way Ryder moved. He pulled the reins back on Cobalt and they slowed to a walk, turned, and headed back to the fence.

"Damn Dante. He's a wild one," Mr. Kensington said through clenched teeth.

"Are you boarding him, or is he yours?"

"Oh, no. We're boarding him, but the owners didn't tell me he hadn't been completely broken yet. I charge a lot more up front for that. I've broken plenty of horses, but this one just doesn't want it. He has a free spirit. I think I might let Ryder have a shot with him."

"What do you mean by broken?"

"Breaking a horse is kind of like training a dog. You know, get them used to your commands, and do what you want, when you want it? Except with a horse, it's training them to accept a rider, too not just the commands. Most horses spook out when they have a rider on their back for the first time. You have to go slow with it and be easy with them. If Dante wasn't good on a halter, I wouldn't have taken him. I guess since he seemed okay I figured it wouldn't be a big deal to take him in."

"So what can he do?" Andrew asked.

"Well, he accepts a saddle now, but he doesn't like the bit at all."

All this terminology…Andrew felt like he needed to study a book. What's a bit? He wondered. He sat up straighter, not asking. "And you think Ryder can do it?"

"Yep."

"Can't he get hurt?"

Mr. Kensington looked up at him, his eyes crinkling up with his smile. "Sure he can, but he's smart. He's not an expert at it, but I've seen him work with spooked animals before, and he's pretty good. If he can get Dante to take a rider, well, I think it'll be a damn miracle, but I've run out of other options."

The conversation lulled as Ryder headed back toward them, leading Dante. Andrew kept his eyes focused on Ryder, unable to take his eyes away from his shape. He held on to his reins with one hand, while the other held the lead of Dante. The horse followed after him with no resistance as if he hadn't just been running away. His uncle went ahead to meet them and open one of the gates, but Andrew stayed put.

The cold breeze blew through Ryder's long, brown locks

and they floated on the wind, brushing against his lips. His eyes
sparkled wide with laughter as he handed off the lead to his uncle.
His lean body rolled with each step of his horse, looking more like
an extension of the creature than a separate being. Andrew's pulse
quickened at the sight and he shifted uneasily in the saddle, looking
down at himself in alarm as other things stirred in his body—things
that shouldn't be stirring when he looked at one of his friends. One
of his *male* friends.

What the hell was wrong with him? It had to be the riding.
Sitting in the saddle for so long…it was probably putting pressure
in the exact wrong spot, at the exact wrong time. It had been a while
since he'd gotten laid.

It's natural. Completely fine.

Ryder stopped in front of him and Andrew's focus shifted to
him. He hadn't been paying much attention and didn't realize Ryder
had gotten so close, and from the look on his friend's face, Ryder
knew it. He felt his face heat up but couldn't look away. Ryder's
eyes caught his and seemed to burn through him, looking into his
mind and seeing what he saw, feeling what he felt. The smile that
pulled at his lips hinted at something far from innocent, and Andrew
shivered.

"Let's head back," Ryder whispered and didn't wait for Andrew
to answer. Cobalt turned and walked for the barn. Andrew hesitated
a moment before he and Magpie followed after him.

Together the two of them got the horses tied, removed the
riding gear, and put it away. From the tack room, Ryder pulled out
two buckets of grooming supplies and handed Magpie's to Andrew.
Ryder showed him what to do with Cobalt first, then the mare.
Ryder's hand covered Andrew's over the currycomb, guiding him
into firm but gentle strokes to brush the horse. He barely heard
Ryder's instructions, though; his mind was lost in thought. When
Ryder released his hand, Andrew stopped brushing and stood there,
staring at Magpie's flank.

Why had his body reacted like that to Ryder? Or before, in
the barn, when Ryder brushed against him. It had felt warm and

comfortable, but Andrew knew he shouldn't feel like that. Danielle and Cynthia were warm and comfortable. And soft. Ryder was not soft.

"Andy? You all right, man?"

Distantly he heard his name and turned to face Ryder, then blinked back to the present. "Huh? Oh, yeah. I'm fine. Maybe a little tired. But I had fun."

"Glad you enjoyed it. You should come over Saturday if you're not busy."

"I don't know…my dad might need me," Andrew hedged, unable to shake the feeling that things were suddenly different between the two of them. He couldn't put his finger on it, but it was…something. Maybe he didn't want to know.

"Well, if he doesn't need you, then. We can spend the day out riding. I can show you how to trot. You seem comfortable enough in the saddle. By the way, how do your legs feel?"

"They're all right. My ass is a little sore."

Ryder smirked and gave Magpie a sugar cube from his pocket. "Wait until you start to trot. It's really going to be sore then," he said, leaning against the wall and staring at him with one eyebrow raised.

That same strange feeling spiraled through Andrew. Scowling, he threw the brush at Ryder. "Shut up about my sore ass already."

❖

"Danielle called."

Andrew looked up at Andrea and then down at his math book again. The numbers swam uselessly on the page, taunting him as he tried to wrangle them into some sort of equation.

"She said to tell you she's sorry, she didn't mean it, and would like to hang out on Saturday. She's free."

"She told you all that? Seriously?"

"Actually she told Mom all that. Not me."

"Mom? That's a little much."

"Yeah, well, Mom wants to know why you didn't tell her you

were having girl trouble again. I'm wondering the same thing, actually. Why didn't you tell me? You know I wouldn't have told Mom."

"Because it's none of her business. And I guess I just didn't think it was that important."

"Whatever."

"As if you'd want some guy talking to Mom about you. I didn't like Danielle that much, anyway."

"That's what you said about Cynthia," Andrea teased from her desk. Andrew crumpled a piece of paper and chucked it at her head, but it fell short and dropped onto the carpet in the middle of the room. "You're going to say that about every girl that breaks up with you. Face it. You suck at relationships."

"Like you're any better, Andrea," he said in response. She stuck out her tongue over her shoulder.

"So, are you going to call her back?"

"No, I've got plans on Saturday."

"What plans? You didn't tell me about this."

"It just came up. Ryder's teaching me how to ride a horse. That's where I went after school today."

"Bet you're going to fall off," Andrea said, sipping from a mug of hot chocolate.

"Shut the hell up. I didn't fall, actually." At least, not off a horse. "You're the impulsive one who'd fall off."

Andrea flipped him off as she went back to her homework. A few minutes later, she asked, "Did you hear anything today from Coach about the scouts? Have they set up an appointment yet?"

"No," Andrew replied, giving up on his math as he set the book aside.

"I wish they'd hurry up."

"Nothing may come from it, Andy. Don't get your hopes up."

"You're so damn negative! If you think positive, good things happen. If you don't quit being such a pessimist, you'll ruin our chances."

I don't know if I want the same chances anymore, he thought, but didn't dare voice it. Andrea would kill him if she knew he was, again, thinking about giving up soccer and focusing solely on his education. It had been her—no, their—goal since they made it onto the varsity team their sophomore year. But it wasn't as if he wanted to play soccer professionally. It was just something fun to do after school. He could get other scholarships, academic scholarships. His grades were good enough. Soccer wasn't his whole life. It didn't have to be, did it? Everything in his world seemed to be shifting.

CHAPTER SEVEN

O n Saturday morning Andrew drove out to the Kensingtons'
place after breakfast. The air had a biting chill more intense
than the day before and the sky had grown overcast. A light snow
began to fall and the small flakes drifted lazily to the ground. Andrew
could smell the snow in the air and when he breathed out, he could
see his breath before him.

When he reached the house, he pulled into the driveway and
parked beside another truck with a large horse trailer attached.
Ahead of him, the lights were on in the barn and Mr. Kensington
was talking to a man standing next to him. He waved when he saw
Andrew.

"Ryder's up in his room. He's waiting for you."

"Thanks, Mr. Kensington."

A fire blazed in the living room, making the house warm and
inviting. Andrew waved to Ryder's aunt and headed up the narrow
stairs to the bedroom right at the top. The door stood ajar and Ryder
lay back on his bed, his iPod lying on his chest and the earbuds nestled
in his ears. He didn't seem to notice Andrew as he approached, and
Andrew felt the sudden urge to shove his cold hands against him.
So he did.

Ryder yelled loudly, sitting up with a start. "Damnit, Andy!
You scared me! That's cold!"

"Gotcha." Andrew grinned wickedly. He fell back when a
pillow hit his face.

"Yeah, whatever. You ready?"

"Yup, ready. We're taking Magpie again?"

"Of course," Ryder said, getting up and pulling his boots on. He reached under his bed and pulled out a box. "Here."

Andrew took it, confused. "What's this?"

"For you. Just open it. Consider it your early Christmas present."

"Ryder."

"Just open it. Besides, you need it."

Andrew glared at him and opened the box. Inside, wrapped in white tissue, he found a pair of brown boots, size ten. He pulled them out and held them up, inspecting them while he ran his fingers over the soft leather. *These must have cost a fortune. Why did he get these for me?* He was stunned. "Thanks." He realized his voice had come out slightly breathless, as if he had trouble getting air.

Ryder beamed and shrugged a shoulder, reaching up to pull his hair back into a short ponytail. "I'd like a new iPod Nano for Christmas. The red one," he teased. Andrew considered throwing the boots at him, but didn't. Instead, he sat on the edge of the bed and pulled them on. They were a comfortable fit and not too stiff.

"These are great, Ryder. Thanks."

"Just make sure you come over and ride with me. I don't want them to go to waste."

"I will. I promise." And after Andrew said it, he realized he meant it. In the short time they had been friends, he had come to value Ryder's friendship immensely. Ryder didn't get caught up in the drama like Charlie, Andrea, and Sarah did. He was confident in his own skin.

The two of them made their way out to the barn and both were excited to see a light flurry had begun. The truck with the trailer no longer stood in the driveway.

"There was someone out here with your uncle before. Who was that?"

"Oh, the vet. He came out to take a look at one of the boarded horses. Uncle Kyle must have gone with him to his office. Come on."

Inside the barn, the heaters worked hard to keep it warm and comfortable. Andrew found it easy to forget the cold outside as he and Ryder prepared the horses for a ride.

Andrew remembered a lot from earlier in the week and did most of it on his own. Ryder checked to make sure Andrew had secured the saddle.

"I'm impressed," Ryder commented, nodding as he walked around Magpie. "Most don't remember everything after just one go."

Pleased with himself, Andrew led Magpie to the barn door and pushed it open only to stop in his tracks. Next to him the mare snorted softly and pulled back, stamping her foot against the barn floor.

"What's wrong? Move," Ryder said, coming up behind him. Cobalt nosed his shoulder and pushed him forward.

"We're heading out in that?" Andrew pointed at the thick wall of flakes that fell from the sky, completely whiting out the landscape. The fence to one of the fields could not be seen though it stood only a few yards away from the barn. The trees did not seem to exist anymore. Nothing existed farther than two feet beyond the barn. No sound, no object. Nothing.

"What the hell," Ryder groaned. "It wasn't snowing like this ten minutes ago. That's too much to ride in."

"Maybe it'll pass? We can wait in here, right?"

Ryder seemed to consider, and finally nodded. "Yeah, we can wait it out. Those are big flakes. That means it won't last too long, right? That's what my aunt said."

Andrew nodded. "Sometimes."

The two of them put the horses back in their stalls to wait it out. Andrew pushed himself up on the half door of Magpie's stall and leaned against the wall, his legs resting along the top of the low door. Ryder leaned against it, resting his chin on his arms. Magpie slowly chewed on some of her hay, regarding them with her big brown eyes.

"Danielle called me the other day. While I was here," Andrew finally said, holding up a piece of hay and twirling it between his fingers.

"Oh? What did she want? I thought she broke up with you."

"She did. She apologized and wanted to hang out today."

"But you're here."

"Yeah. I'm here."

Ryder looked up at him. Andrew shredded a piece of hay and picked another off his jeans and began to worry at that one as well. "Didn't want to hang out with her?"

"No. I sort of made plans with you, didn't I?"

"As I recall, you said you'd think about it. That your dad might need you."

Andrew lifted a hand and gestured vaguely. "Well, he didn't, so I'm here. Besides. I didn't really like her. She was on the way to being as needy as Cynthia, I could tell. Better to end it now and not have to deal with the drama later."

"So who do you have in mind now?"

Silence filled the air as Andrew pondered that question. After what seemed like an eternity waiting, he felt Ryder shift his gaze up to him. *Who do I have in mind? Who do I have in mind? Is there anyone left?* That question made him cringe.

"No one," he said finally, feeling confused at his own words. "I hadn't even given it thought."

"Maybe you need to take some time off from the serial dating. Just hang with the guys, yeah?"

"Maybe." Andrew thought about it, and the idea of not having to meet anyone's expectations but his own appealed to him.

The silence resumed for another few minutes, and it was neither comfortable nor strained, but an odd mix of the two. Andrew felt like Ryder had something to say to him. He wanted to ask him, but he didn't know how to. Magpie wandered over after eating and nudged his thigh with her velvety nose. He lifted a hand to stroke it gently, enjoying the smooth texture and contemplating his next words.

"So…speaking of girls, you said you were already interested in someone when I told you Sarah wanted you. Who is it?"

"Andy…" Ryder hesitated. Magpie turned her head to sniff Andrew's pockets, looking for a treat. "It's complicated."

"Why? Is she already dating someone?"

"Well, no."

"Then how could it be complicated?" Andrew asked. He pushed Magpie's nose away from its quest.

"You're my friend, right?"

The sudden, random question startled Andrew and he nearly fell off the wall into Magpie's stall. The horse shied away from them warily and moved her attentions elsewhere. Andrew looked at Ryder to see if he was serious, and found him staring back, his face carefully blank. *What the hell kind of question is that?* "Of course I'm your friend. Hell, I've been hanging out with you more than I have with Charlie."

"Even if I were to tell you a secret that…most people around here probably wouldn't agree with? You'd still want to hang out?"

"You're a cool guy, Ryder. We're cool."

"Even if your other friends thought—" Ryder pressed his lips together.

Andrew wondered what the big secret was. And what wouldn't his friends like? "Well, as long as you haven't, like, murdered someone or gotten my sister pregnant, I don't think there's much you could say that would make me stop wanting to hang out with you." He paused and then looked at him closely with squinted eyes, a little nervous. "You haven't killed someone, right?"

Ryder laughed softly and shook his head. "No, it's nothing like that." When he looked up at him, a serious expression settled across his face. "Remember when you said Sarah liked me, and I said she wasn't my type?"

"I remember. Why?" he asked suspiciously. Sarah was pretty. Gorgeous, really, he supposed, though she had been his friend for so long he couldn't see her that way. She could be any guy's type of girl: funny, smart, sporty but feminine, and beautiful.

Ryder took a deep breath and breathed out before speaking softly. "She's not my type because she's a girl. I like guys, Andy. I'm…gay."

Andrew stared at him in complete shock over his confession. Well…that wasn't what he was expecting. He looked at the wall, then back at Ryder, and back again to the wall, trying to gather his thoughts. What came out was simply a soft "oh."

"Oh? That's it?"

"Yeah, oh." When he really stopped and thought about it, Andrew wasn't surprised. Not like he would've been if the secret had been, say, Charlie's. And something about the admission made him feel strange. Excited. He didn't know what that meant.

"So...we're cool?" Ryder finally asked, looking nervous for the first time since Andrew had met him.

Andrew nodded and flashed him a small grin. "Yeah, we're cool."

Ryder visibly relaxed.

"So, uh...when did you know?"

"That I was gay?" Andrew nodded and Ryder focused on the far wall as if recalling a distant memory. "I started to realize I was different at thirteen, but I knew for sure once I hit fourteen."

"That early?"

"Yep. There was this girl in class that all my friends were pushing me to go out with. I wasn't really interested in her. I mean, she wasn't that cute, but I did it anyway. We went to the movies and then for ice cream. She kind of jumped on me and kissed me at the end, and pushed herself close up against me. It just felt...wrong. Like, disgusting."

"Wow."

"Yeah. And I realized after that, well, I didn't want what she had to offer. But my friend, Jason, on the other hand, did."

"Did you and Jason...you know, date or anything?"

"Hell no. Jason is straight. He'd probably have punched me if he knew what I actually thought about him. He didn't care when I told him, though. As long as I didn't hit on him, or do anything really 'gay' in front of him, whatever that means. He said it opened up more opportunities for him with the ladies."

They laughed about it, and Andrew relaxed back against the wall. "Did you ever date a guy?" He felt oddly at ease talking about this with Ryder.

"Oh, sure. Plenty of times. Had a serious boyfriend for a while.

Well, as serious as you can get when you're sixteen. Name was Kevin Anders. Our fathers knew each other from the military, and he lived over in the next town. Another military brat. We hung out all the time. Messed around. Until his mother caught us."

"She caught you? Doing what?" Andrew asked, horrified at the thought of any mother catching her son having sex whether they were gay or straight.

"What do you think? We were having sex. It was the most awkward moment of my life, I can tell you. If I ever get hard and need it to go away fast, I just think about that moment and it's gone like that," he said, snapping his fingers.

Andrew's heart thumped at the idea of Ryder getting hard.

"I had gone over to his house after school and we were supposed to be there alone. We were in his room, just getting into it and she came home. We didn't hear her, so when she pushed his door open…" He shrugged and looked up at Andrew.

Andrew watched him, intrigued. "What did she do?"

"Told me to get out of her house and not come back. She said she wouldn't tell our fathers if we didn't see each other anymore. So we didn't."

"Just like that? You didn't see him anymore?"

"Are you dense, man? Both of our fathers are in the military! We'd have been kicked out of our houses, shipped off to boot camp to straighten us out, or worse! I wasn't going to mess with that. Ever hear of Don't Ask, Don't Tell? It might not be around anymore, but it sure as hell still existed then."

Andrew could not imagine what it would be like to be caught or to have to tell his parents. "I wouldn't be able to tell my dad," he said after a moment. "I know that. He's cool, but that would be too much for him."

"Yeah, it's hard. My parents don't know. I mean, I'm sure my mom might suspect it. But she's never asked, and I won't tell. I know she wouldn't tell my dad even if she did know, though."

"Have you…dated anyone since you've been up here?"

Ryder laughed and shook his head. "No. I haven't been looking."

"You said before that you had someone in mind, but not Sarah," Andrew said, unable to keep the topic from drifting back to that. *Who is it he likes? It can't be Josh Grayson. But who else is there?* He tried to picture others in their school but failed. Andrew watched Ryder as he hesitated again and looked up at him. The teasing was gone from his voice when he answered.

"I do have someone in mind. But…right now, I don't think I should do anything about it. I don't want to screw anything up if I'm wrong, you know? It can be hard. Sometimes you fall for someone straight, and it sucks."

Though Andrew felt a little disappointment, he nodded. He couldn't quite pinpoint why he felt disappointed. Because Ryder wouldn't tell him which guy he'd been watching? It wasn't any of his business if Ryder didn't want to share. But they'd been hanging out so much, it felt like Ryder would tell him before he'd tell anyone else.

Oh well.

Andrew shrugged it off and they talked idly for another thirty minutes before the snow finally slowed enough for them to go out. As they walked out into the silent, late morning, Ryder dropped a hand on his shoulder.

"Thanks for listening. It felt good to get it off my chest."

"Anytime, Ryder. It's really okay."

❖

The boys rode in from the field after two hours of riding to warm up and get something to eat. Andrew's body ached in places he never thought possible, and Ryder teased him mercilessly as Andrew slid off Magpie and stumbled.

"And you thought you had strong legs." He laughed, still sitting astride Cobalt. Magpie nickered softly and nudged Andrew's back pocket. He pulled out a sugar cube and held it out for her.

"She's going to get fat with all the sugar she eats," Andrew said.

"And you're changing the subject yet again."

Ryder dismounted more gracefully than Andrew had, prompting a slight twinge of jealousy. Even though Ryder had been riding forever, and this was only his second day, he still hated being shown up.

"You're doing really well with guiding the horse, but your form when you trot? It sucks. You bounce all over the saddle. You're going to fall off if you go any faster."

"Shut up," Andrew responded as they put the riding gear back in the tack room and headed inside.

"I'm trying to help!"

Mrs. Kensington stood in the kitchen again, adding some spices to a soup when they stomped in. "Boots. Off," she commanded before they could track mud into the rest of the house. They sat on the floor and pulled the boots off, dumped them at the door, and then ran up to Ryder's room.

"We can go back out for another ride later," Ryder said, flopping back on his bed. Andrew sat on the edge of it gingerly; clothes and books littered the desk chair, preventing him from taking a seat there. "The horses need a rest."

"Screw the horses. I need a rest. My ass is sore."

Ryder snorted and grabbed a pillow. He pulled it against him and curled up on his side. "Think Andrea would like riding?"

"I don't know. She might. She likes horses, but never asked for lessons."

"Is she feeling better?"

"Better enough to be a witch about Danielle." And continue bothering him about college plans. She needed to lay off.

"Isn't that the job of a sister?" Ryder nudged him with his foot.

"Yeah, I guess it is."

Ryder's room was directly over the kitchen, and they could smell the fresh bread baking in the stove. The room itself, aside from the messy desk and chair, was clean and neat with light brown walls. The comforter and pillows on the bed were black, and the rest of the furniture was cherry-stained pine. On the desk sat Ryder's computer, the screen black. A stack of CDs balanced next to it, with crumpled paper scattered across the top. A few more sheets made it into the small garbage can under the desk.

Andrew noticed the bookcase in the corner, stuffed completely with books of all sizes. "Are all of those yours?"

"Yeah. Brought them up with me."

"I didn't know you liked to read. I've never seen you read outside of class."

"Well, when we're hanging out, would you want me to sit there and do nothing but read?" Andrew didn't have to think about it and shook his head. "There you go."

Ryder pushed himself up on one elbow, resting his head in his hand, with the other arm draped over the pillow. Andrew glanced back at him but didn't say anything; he looked on the verge of revealing something.

"Andrew," he started, tongue darting out to lick his lips, "have you ever…have you ever kissed a guy?"

"N-no. Of course not." Andrew snorted and flicked his glance toward the firmly shut door. He could hear Mrs. Kensington moving around in the kitchen, a cabinet door slammed shut and the sound echoed up the stairwell.

"Of course not," Ryder repeated, softly, shaking his head. He sat up, gaze locked with Andrew's.

"I'm…I'm not…"

"No, of course you aren't."

The moment stilled.

Without meaning to, Andrew leaned a little closer. His skin felt hot, tight.

Ryder didn't say anything as he moved forward. He placed his warm hand lightly on Andrew's cheek. Andrew leaned into the touch, his lips parting slightly, waiting for Ryder to make a move. When he did, Andrew moved closer to him, hesitating. With his face just a few inches from Ryder's, Andrew licked his lips. He felt his cheeks flame. Ryder leaned forward a little more, their lips almost brushing. It wouldn't take anything more than a tip of his head to close that distance. "Andrew…" Ryder started, his breath gently brushing Andrew's lips.

A knock at the door sent them reeling from each other. When it opened a second later, Ryder's aunt popped her head into the room to find the boys on opposite sides of the bed, Andrew's legs drawn up against his chest and arms clutched around them. "Is…everything all right?" she asked, frowning.

"Yes. We're fine," Ryder answered for them, an easy grin on his face. Inside, though, Andrew felt like he'd been a naughty little boy with his hand caught in the cookie jar.

"Okay. I just wanted to let you boys know lunch is ready when you want it."

"Thanks, Aunt Lisa. We'll be right down."

She hesitated a moment before pulling the door shut after her. Both boys breathed a huge sigh of relief once it clicked and her footsteps sounded on the stairs.

All of Andrew's nerves fired at once. He'd gotten caught up in a moment he didn't understand. "Maybe I should go," Andrew started.

Ryder caught his hand. "Stay. Please. I'm sorry about that just now. I thought—"

"Let's not talk about it right now, okay?"

"But you'll stay?" Ryder asked, a hint of worry in his voice.

Andrew's pulse raced and his mind reeled from their near kiss. "Don't you think my staying would…make it more awkward?"

"No, I don't."

Andrew frowned. "All right…I'll stay. At least for lunch," he added, not promising to stay any longer. "But I don't…I don't know what just happened."

"It's okay." Ryder sighed and sat up, brushing a hand through his hair. They both headed downstairs to the kitchen, silent. Ryder teased his aunt when he saw her and sat at the table, acting as if nothing happened, while Andrew felt tense and nervous. Every look Mrs. Kensington gave him set alarms screaming in his mind.

Does she know what just happened?

No, how could she?

Does she maybe suspect something?

Is she looking at me different?

Impossible.

She knows we're just friends.

Nothing to suspect, right?

Wait, do his aunt and uncle know he's gay?

When Ryder's foot accidentally bumped against his under the table, he nearly jumped out of his skin.

"Are you all right, Andrew?" Mrs. Kensington asked, concern showing in her hazel eyes. Andrew nodded and started to speak, but Ryder cut him off.

"Of course he's all right!" Ryder looked pointedly at Andrew. "You're all right, right?"

"Right."

"He's just anxious to get back out and ride." Ryder pushed away from the table and stood. Andrew followed him.

"Yes. Anxious. Thanks for lunch, Mrs. Kensington."

"Anytime, Andrew," she smiled, taking their bowls away with hers and watching as they pulled on their boots and jackets and headed out to the barn.

The air outside was even quieter than before. From the short storm a few hours earlier, three inches of fresh snow covered the ground, and their steps crunched it down. The barn was filled with warm air and the scent of hay and horse. Cobalt and Magpie seemed to know they were going out again and were waiting for them, their heads peering out of their stalls.

The boys worked in silence, Andrew lost in his own thoughts. The few times Ryder looked over at him, Andrew's mind raced. So much going through his head, his eyes stared at the horse but didn't really see her. The start of a battle raged in his mind, and every time his thoughts started to make sense, images of Ryder's lips so close to his came flooding back. He tried to shut down his visions, but couldn't. If he tried to redirect them, the images just came back.

Ryder had almost kissed him. His lips…so close.

Why had he done that?

Why did I lean toward him? I was just curious. That's all.

Ryder's aunt had prevented anything from really happening.

Nothing really would have happened. Really. But their lips had been so close…

Ryder cleared his throat and Andrew looked up, stunned. Once again Ryder stood just inches away, and Andrew took a step back. Which put him directly against one of the stall doors. "Ryder…"

Whatever he wanted to say was lost as Ryder closed the distance, not giving him any time to protest, and sealed their lips together. Andrew's body tensed momentarily, then relaxed when he felt Ryder's hand wrap around his forearm. The other pressed against the wall by his shoulder, supporting his body as he leaned into Andrew.

Andrew's eyes shut, his brain reeled…and he returned the kiss.

Ryder slid his hand down to rest against Andrew's hip. He took a step closer to him and their bodies pressed together. The sudden contact broke the trance that held Andrew and he pushed Ryder away, hauling in a noisy breath of air in the process.

Too much, his mind screamed at him. *Too much!*

"Andy? Are you okay? I…I didn't…" Ryder swept his hand through his hair. "Look, I'm sorry. No, that's not true. I'm not sorry. Are you…okay?" Ryder tilted his head to the side and leaned over to bring himself nearly eye level with Andrew.

"I'm fine," Andrew insisted, waving a hand. "Fine. I gotta go, though."

"But I thought—"

"I just have to get home, okay? I'll…call you tomorrow?"

"Andy, I didn't mean to—"

"I can't talk about this right now." He held up both palms. "I need to think. I need time to think." And he couldn't do it here. Not with Ryder so close and his lips so soft and…

Stop. Don't think about it right now, Andrew. Just go home.

Ryder's face fell, but he nodded agreement. "Okay."

Andrew stepped around Ryder and headed for the house where he'd left his jacket. He traded his boots for his sneakers, thankful Mrs. Kensington wasn't around for him to have to explain anything to. When he took off in his truck, he glanced in the rearview mirror and saw Ryder standing in the open barn door, watching him drive away. Just before he came to the bend in the road, Ryder disappeared back inside.

"Damnit!" Andrew yelled in the quiet of the cab.

What in the hell just happened?

CHAPTER EIGHT

By the time Andrew got home that night, his entire body ached from riding and his mind still raced from the kiss. He'd driven around town before turning onto the back roads and following them while his mind tried to sort itself out. After two hours, he had made absolutely no progress; he was just as confused as before.

Why had Ryder kissed him? Why hadn't he pushed Ryder away the second he got closer? Why had he waited until Ryder had actually put his hands on him?

Why did it feel so damn good?

"What's wrong with you?" Andrea asked as he settled onto the couch.

"We were riding all day," he lied. "God, I'm sore," he groaned, letting his head drop back onto the overstuffed cushion. His father chuckled as he stepped into the room and took a seat in his armchair with a cup of coffee.

"I suggest you go take a hot shower, or you're going to be stiff tomorrow."

"That's a really good idea. Thanks, Dad."

"You're welcome."

"You don't plan on going back there again tomorrow, do you?" his sister asked.

"No," he said, shaking his head. There was no way he could face Ryder so soon. "Why?"

Andrea shrugged. "Charlie called earlier. He wanted to know

if you wanted to go catch a movie. I thought maybe I'd bring Sarah along, and you can invite Ryder, too, if you want."

Too soon. "Maybe I'll call Ryder and see if he wants to join us, too," he said, though he wasn't sure if he should after what happened between them. But wouldn't it seem strange to not invite him along?

Andrea hesitated and Andrew stopped his slow progress up the steps, backing down them a bit.

"Andrea, what is it?"

"Charlie asked if it could just be the four of us. You know, like old times."

Andrew stared at her, confused. "Why would he ask that?"

"I don't know. I'm just telling you what he told me, okay?"

"Seems weird. Ryder's our friend, too. What does it matter?"

"Maybe he just thinks you're spending more time with Ryder than you are with him. Which you have been, I noticed. Charlie is your best friend, isn't he?"

"Of course he is. He's just being an idiot lately. Besides, he's the one that hasn't asked to do anything since soccer season ended. It goes both ways." Andrew paused. "Did he tell you that's what he thought?"

"No, of course not. Charlie wouldn't actually talk about it. You know him. I said *maybe* that's what he thinks." She held up her hands. "Don't shoot the messenger. Go take a shower, then call him," she added, with a wrinkle of her nose, "you smell like a barn."

"I was in one, genius."

"That's enough, you two," their father said, throwing them both a stern look.

Tossing a last frown over his shoulder, Andrew climbed the stairs to the small bathroom and slipped inside. Once in the small space, the scent of horse, hay, and manure nearly overwhelmed him. And reminded him of Ryder. He quickly shed his clothes and shoved them in the hamper, then turned on the water and stepped inside the shower, shutting the curtain.

The hot water felt great on his back as it slid down his body. He relaxed under the hot spray and let it wash away the tension in his body and clear his mind. Grabbing his shampoo and soap, he rinsed the smell of horse and hay from his body. When he finished he felt a lot better than before and could ignore the noises clamoring in his mind.

After he climbed out of the shower and wrapped his towel around his waist he realized he hadn't brought any clean clothes into the bathroom with him. Darting across the hall, he shut the bedroom door behind him, grabbed a clean pair of sweats and a T-shirt. Once dressed, he felt a little warmer and flopped on his bed with his phone.

He dialed Charlie's number while he lay there, and while waiting for him to answer, he inspected his hand. Though he'd worn gloves, parts of his palms were rubbed raw from holding the reins too tightly.

"Hello?" Charlie's voice came through his cell phone, clear as if he stood right next to him in the room.

"Hey, Charlie. It's me."

"Hey, Andy. What's up?"

"Andrea said you called and wanted to see a movie tomorrow."

"Yeah! Glad you got the message. I wasn't sure if she'd tell you or not. She was rude as hell earlier. She wants to bring Sarah along. That would be cool, right?"

"That's fine," Andrew said, before adding, cautiously after Andrea's words earlier, "We should bring Ryder, too."

Silence filled the line as Charlie paused and Andrew pulled his phone away to see if he lost service. "Let's go with just the four of us. We can bring Ryder next time."

"Why not this time?"

"Look, I just don't want to, okay?"

"Does this have anything to do with Sarah? He's not interested in her, man. You're fine."

"I know that! It's not that, all right? I just want to hang out like we did before."

Andrew laughed into the phone. "You sound like a jealous girlfriend."

"Shut up, ass. I'm not a fag."

The tone of his voice when he said it made Andrew stop abruptly, and his laughter died. What would Charlie think if he knew about Ryder? What would he think if he knew what had happened between them in the barn? Would those same words, that same tone, be directed at him?

"So? Are we on, or what?"

"You know what? I'll think about it," Andrew said, and hung up the phone without saying good-bye. He stared up at the ceiling in disbelief. Something else was bothering Charlie, and he'd been spending too much time with Ryder to notice. It could be that Charlie was jealous. Ryder had quickly become popular, and all the girls in the school were constantly hanging around him. Yeah, he flirted with them when they were around, but now that he knew his secret, Andrew knew Charlie had nothing to worry about. But Charlie didn't know that.

He couldn't do anything about it until they hung out tomorrow. If they did. He pulled back the covers on his bed and crawled into the cold sheets. They warmed up a short time later, but he couldn't rest. He lay in bed staring at the ceiling for what seemed like hours, replaying the kiss in his mind, over and over. Even now he could still feel the press of those warm, soft lips against his. He licked his. Ryder had tasted like the Chapstick he wore while riding: a smooth and light mint taste. And just a little like what they'd eaten for lunch. Even though the kiss had been brief—*too brief, and that was my fault*, he thought—it still sent a jolt straight down his spine just thinking about it. Ryder hadn't been pushy or demanding. Instead, he clearly knew what he was doing, and it was good. Better than what he'd gotten from the girls lately, and all in a simple kiss. A simple kiss that had left him breathless and looking like an idiot.

Andrew lay there in the bed until his mother called him down for a late dinner. His mind still raced through the afternoon, reliving each and every moment they were together. He could hardly push his thoughts aside while he ate with his family, not wanting to reveal what troubled him, but he managed well enough. They hardly seemed to notice, though Andrea eyed him suspiciously a few times and nudged his foot under the table. He ignored her. And that night when they were in their beds, long after she'd fallen asleep, he still lay there staring at the wall, mind full of Ryder and their kiss.

Ryder had surprised him when he'd admitted he was gay.

He'd surprised him with the kiss.

But the biggest surprise of all? Andrew wanted to kiss him again.

CHAPTER NINE

Charlie was still talking about the movie they had seen Sunday afternoon at lunchtime on Monday. He settled into the chair across from Andrew and took a bite from his slice of pizza. Sarah made a face when a piece of crust fell from his lips and he started to talk. Again.

"Ugh, close your mouth when you chew, Charlie. That's disgusting."

"Yeah," Andrea said, sitting next to Andrew. "Really. Should I have worn my rain jacket to lunch today?"

Andrew bit into his sandwich, nodding. "I think you should have."

"Thanks for the warning," she muttered.

"Hey guys, how was the movie?" Ryder asked as he sat down next to Andrew. If he felt Andrew tense beside him, he didn't seem to pay any attention to it.

"Great, and Charlie won't shut up about it," Sarah said with a bright smile on her face. Despite Ryder repeatedly turning her down, her interest still shone clearly on her face. If the gleam in her eyes meant anything, she wouldn't give up on him anytime soon. Andrew almost wanted to laugh. If she only knew.

"Really? Why? What happened?" Ryder asked, fixing his green-eyed gaze on Charlie, who stopped talking and focused on his food. The sudden silence at their table deafened Andrew.

When no one said anything, Ryder looked at Andrew, confused. "Did I miss something?"

"No," he said, shaking his head. "I'll tell you about the movie later."

Ryder nodded. "You coming over after school?"

Andrew nodded. "Sure."

Charlie muttered something and stood, leaving his food half-eaten on his tray. Sarah scowled after him as he left. "He's had such an attitude since Saturday. I don't know what the hell his problem is, but if he doesn't knock it off, I'll kick his ass myself."

Andrea rolled her eyes and leaned against her elbows on the table. "Oh yeah, I'm sure you can take him on."

"What? He won't hit a girl. And I'll aim straight for his balls," she said with a wink. "Instant knockout." The girls laughed.

Andrew noticed Ryder trying to catch his attention and he looked away. He knew he would ask what was going on, but he didn't know how to answer it. He wasn't even sure of the answer himself. And he didn't want to get into it in front of Sarah and Andrea. *It would just lead to uncomfortable questions, and I'm not ready for that.*

The rest of the lunch period was strained. When it finally ended, Ryder caught Andrew's arm and held him back. The crowd pushed around them to file back to their classes.

"Andy—"

"We can't talk about this now. I'll tell you after school. Meet us at my truck, okay?" Ryder nodded, and Andrew walked away.

He could feel Ryder's hot gaze on his back the whole way.

❖

As Andrea and Andrew approached the truck, Andrew saw Ryder waiting for them. Andrea squeezed into the middle of the seat and complained about it, but her complaints fell on deaf ears. An awkward silence fell over the truck during the drive home, even worse than the silence at the lunch table, and Andrea seemed to sense it.

"Wow, this has been lovely," she said in a wry tone when they pulled into their driveway, climbing over Ryder to get out of the cab without waiting for him to get out first. She ran inside with a small, dismissive wave over her shoulder.

"Talk," Ryder said as Andrew backed the truck out of his driveway and headed for the Kensingtons' farm.

"I'm sorry I didn't invite you to the movie, okay? I wanted to, but Charlie threw a fit about it. He was pissed that I've been hanging out with you more than him."

"Really?" Ryder frowned and looked out the window as they passed a snow-covered field.

"Yeah. Like I said, I'm sorry."

"Don't worry, it's fine. I had stuff to do in the barn on Sunday anyway."

Andrew wondered if Ryder was just trying to make him feel better. "Okay."

"Charlie can come over too, if he really wants to. He just didn't seem like he'd be interested."

Andrew sighed. "I don't think it's that. He's jealous. I know that."

"Jealous?" Ryder snorted. "Of what?"

"You?"

"Because of you?"

"No, no. Nothing like that." But Andrew's heart pumped harder just thinking of it. "Sarah hangs all over your every word. Don't say you turned her down," Andrew said, holding up one hand while the other gripped the steering wheel tightly. "I know, and he knows. But she still makes her interest clear, and Charlie gets annoyed. And then there are all the other girls that follow you around."

"Yeah? So what? You know better than any of them why I haven't asked any of them out."

The reminder of Saturday's kiss put color on his cheeks and he stared intently at the road. "I know," he finally said, softly.

"So..."

"So," Andrew responded and left it at that.

They rode in silence for longer this time, and Andrew began to drum his fingers against the wheel. He pulled up to a stop sign and sat there, despite the clear roads. Ryder scanned the roads, and then looked at him, a question in his eyes.

"I thought a lot about that kiss," Andrew finally blurted out. "Shit, it's all I've been able to think about. And...God, I don't know, Ryder. It's ridiculous. I don't know how I feel."

"But you're not disgusted," Ryder pointed out, leaning toward him.

"No, I'm not at all disgusted," he said.

Ryder just let the words hang in the silence of the truck cab.

"I don't know. I don't know what to do. If I should do anything. I shouldn't. I mean, it was just an experiment, right?" He flicked a glance at Ryder.

No answer.

"Right? Curiosity. It happens. And it wasn't bad; I liked it, and that's fine. It doesn't mean anything."

"No?"

"Kisses don't have to mean anything," he lied.

"But sometimes they do."

Andrew expelled a breath. "Ryder, I just don't—"

"Look, Andy, we could go slowly. Just give this a shot and see where it goes." The silence ticked by. "We don't have to tell anyone."

Andrew gripped and released the steering wheel. Gripped and released. Gripped and released. "I've never, you know, dated a guy before." *What am I saying? Am I actually considering this?*

"Obviously," Ryder teased, the sparkle back in his eyes.

"I'm not gay," Andrew argued softly.

"But it's not exactly working out with the girls, is it?"

How could he argue that? Ryder did have a point. "No...it's not."

"So maybe you are, maybe you're not. Maybe you're bisexual. Maybe you just haven't had enough experiences in life to know what you want."

"That's a lot of maybes."

"Life is a lot of maybes."

"Don't most people know what they are?"

Ryder nodded. "Most do, but not all."

Andrew hesitated and bit his lip. He glanced out the window to his side, the roads still clear. He twisted to look back at Ryder but found he couldn't meet his eyes, so he focused instead on the windshield. It was safe enough. He considered all the options. "We wouldn't have to do anything I didn't want?"

"I wouldn't ask you to. We don't even have to 'date.' We could just...see each other."

"We see each other every day."

"It's different."

"Yes, it is."

"So? What do you think? You know, no pressure. Nothing exclusive if you didn't want it to be."

The back of Andrew's neck prickled. "You're going to see other guys?"

Ryder smiled, so gently that Andrew's chest squeezed. "No, Andrew. I'm not."

They sat at the sign through the entirety of an obnoxiously cheerful country song about young love before Andrew pulled away and continued the drive to the farm. It stood just on the other side of a little rise, and already he could see smoke from the chimney. Abruptly, Andrew cut the wheel and pulled off the side of the road. He glanced around to make sure no one could see them and then pinned his gaze on Ryder, who stared back at him with wide eyes.

Andrew's heart slammed against his chest, nearly ready to burst from his body.

"All right."

"All right?" Ryder tilted his head to the side.

Andrew nodded once. "We'll do this. We can 'see' each other or whatever we call it, and see where it goes."

"You're sure? You're serious?"

Andrew eased out a breath. "Yes, I'm serious."

A slow grin pulled at Ryder's face, but it flicked out and he turned serious a second later. "What made you decide this?"

"Like I said, I've thought a lot about the kiss. What we did didn't really bother me. I thought that it should have, but to be honest, it didn't." He cut his gaze to the floor for a moment. "Okay, more than that. It was…good. And I thought about Cynthia and Danielle and how they didn't work out, how dating never works out for me. Maybe this won't either. But I don't know. And…I want to know. What I felt was enough to make this worth giving a shot. Okay?"

"And you're sure you're not doing this just for the hell of it? You're absolutely serious? You won't cry foul later if you decide being with a guy isn't your thing?"

"Yeah. I am. And no," he said with a small, breathless laugh, "I won't cry foul." Andrew checked the mirrors again and leaned toward Ryder. And then kissed him. Ryder leaned into it and put his hand on the back of Andrew's head, pulling him closer. Only when Andrew pressed a hand to his chest did Ryder let go.

"Damn," Andrew said in a shaky tone, turning his attention to the wheel and pulling back onto the road. His cheeks were several degrees hotter than the rest of his skin. His hands were trembling as they clutched at the steering wheel and he thanked God he didn't have to drive much farther.

Seeing where this went with Ryder? Yeah. Yeah, he was sure.

❖

"That's it!" Ryder cried, pulling Cobalt alongside Magpie.

They were in the west field, and after Andrew had finally stayed in his seat while trotting, Ryder convinced him to put more pressure on the horse's sides. The mare had taken off at a gentle run, and after an initial near fall, Andrew managed to stay on.

Laughing along with Ryder, Andrew let out a whoop and held on tightly with his legs. Beneath him the horse rocked, his body moving in sync with hers.

"You're really catching on fast," Ryder called. He motioned for him to slow down and Andrew reluctantly did.

"That was the biggest rush," Andrew replied breathlessly, eyes wide with delight. "Let's go again!" he yelled, turning Magpie around and kicking her into a canter. Andrew rode ahead of Ryder for a while as they headed back to the barn, but he knew Ryder was going easy on him. Ryder was so skilled in the saddle, there was no way Andrew could actually win against him in a race. His suspicions were confirmed when Cobalt overtook Magpie in a sudden burst of speed.

Andrew yelled as Ryder burst ahead of him. He glared with good humor as they dismounted.

"You cheated."

"How did I cheat?" Ryder teased. "I won, fair and square."

"Yeah, but you were letting me win until the end!"

"Would I do that?"

They brought the horses into the barn, groomed them, and set them free in their stalls. Andrew leaned against the wall and watched the mare sampling the grains in her feed bucket. He tensed when Ryder's body leaned up against his. Frowned when Ryder's lips brushed into his hair.

"Ryder..."

"Mmm?"

"Could you...not do that? It's weird."

"Sorry." Ryder stepped back and leaned against the wall, looking up at the rafters.

"Taking things slowly, remember?"

"I remember. I know this is really, really new to you. I'm just... excited."

"I know."

They watched the horses in silence for a few minutes, before Andrew worked up the nerve to reach out and take his hand. The two of them stood that way for a long time; Andrew leaning up against the stall door, Ryder with his back to the wall, still staring at the rafters. The sensation was new, but comfortable, and at that moment Andrew didn't doubt the decision he'd made to give Ryder a chance.

"I'm excited, too," he said softly. Too softly for Ryder to hear, he thought, until that piercing green gaze met his.

CHAPTER TEN

Thanksgiving had always been a busy affair at the Morris household, and this year would be no exception. Andrew's maternal grandparents came down every year to join them, as well as his father's brother, Richard. Though it seemed like there weren't many people, they were loud, and the area they usually hung around in had limited space. After their late lunch, his grandfather, father, and uncle would gather in the living room for the game. Usually one or two of the neighbors would stop by and bring beer.

Reds, golds, and yellows decorated the dining room. The tablecloth added to the theme with a dark yellow color, and a red runner ran down the center. The napkins had little harvest scenes imprinted on them that matched the plastic cornucopia his father had picked up a few years ago at a craft store. At the time, Andrew's mother had thought it tacky, but it had soon become the staple centerpiece to the table—before the turkey, anyway.

That year, his mother had made most of the dinner, and his grandparents brought an assortment of pies and desserts. Andrew sat at the table after dinner finished, staring at the desecrated remains of the turkey, the empty dishes of mashed potatoes, turnips, squash, corn, and green bean casserole. A single piece of pumpkin pie remained, and he eyed it, shifting a bit to see if he had any room left. Just the thought of putting another bite anywhere near his mouth in the next, oh, three days sent his stomach rolling dangerously. He groaned and flopped over.

"That's what you get for overstuffing yourself, Andy," his

grandmother teased, knocking his head lightly with a wooden spoon. He reached up to make sure there wasn't any food residue in his hair.

"But it was so good," he said, in a reverent voice. She laughed and leaned down, kissing his cheek.

"You never could say no to Grandma's pumpkin pie. Any word yet on which college you're going to?"

Andrea passed through the room and grabbed the last roll out of the basket and broke it apart, eating it with relish in front of him. She raised her eyebrow as if expecting to get in on this discussion about their college plans, but the ringing of the doorbell saved him from having to answer.

"I'll get it. It's probably Sarah," Andrea called, and stepped into the hallway. He heard the door open and the muffled sound of voices in the entryway. Someone laughed and boots stomped on the ground.

"No word yet, Grandma. We haven't decided. It's a tough choice."

"Make sure you let us know when you do," she said, patting his hand.

Andrew recognized the voices as they trailed past the door to the dining room and into the living room where the football game was just about to start. There were hellos and other greetings exchanged, and then the snap of beer cans being opened. Andrew started to stand when a hand dropped down over his eyes from behind. He smiled.

"Guess who."

"What do I get if I win?" he asked slyly.

"Oh, I don't know. A surprise? Maybe a piece of pecan pie?"

Andrew groaned, his stomach protesting. "No more food, Ryder. I'll explode." He pushed the hand off his face and stared up into the face above him.

"Yes, we don't want him to explode, so don't feed him anything else, please," Andrew's mother said from the kitchen.

"Happy Thanksgiving, Mrs. Morris," Ryder said. His aunt already hovered in the kitchen, adding her pie to the counter decorated with desserts.

"You too, Ryder, thank you. Why don't you boys go watch the football game in the other room?"

"I'm not really into football," Ryder admitted.

"Finally, someone else who doesn't think it's the only thing in the world that matters on Thanksgiving," Andrew said, not bothering to hide his pleasure.

"You wouldn't think so," his mother teased, "soccer player."

His grandmother laughed and fussed over the new pie. "This looks delicious!" Her voice faded as Andrew stood and tugged Ryder over to the stairs.

"Let's go to my room. Maybe we won't go deaf from the—"

Someone yelled *"Touchdown!"* from the living room. Half the room cheered while the other half groaned loudly. Jeers were called from one side to the other.

"I see your point." Ryder grimaced. "Is this some sort of tradition?"

"Yeah. My grandparents and uncle always come down for the day. We eat. Overeat. Then eat some more. And then the television is turned on and nothing is allowed on but the games."

"Games? Plural?"

"Oh yeah. They'll watch at least two, three games while they're here."

"Damn. I didn't realize that many games were on today."

"Yeah. I'm glad you're here, though. I'd be forced to watch them if you weren't," he said with relief threading through his tone. Ryder clapped a hand on his shoulder.

Cool air flowed out from the bedroom when Andrew pushed the door open, and he paused at the thermostat to adjust it higher. Ryder looked around the room and took in the two beds, his face puzzled. One side of the room was neat and organized while the other had clothes on the floor and makeup on the dresser.

"You share a room with Andrea?"

Andrew sat down on his bed and looked around at the messy side, realizing he'd never really talked about his unfortunate bunking situation with Ryder. "Yeah. Temporarily. Dad started putting new hardwood floors in the house, and they ran out of supplies halfway through mine. That wouldn't be so bad, but the walls had to be gutted in my room when the roof leaked. So I moved into Andrea's room on a long-term, temporary basis?" He shrugged. "The roof, at least, has been fixed, and Dad said they're finishing it this winter, but I don't mind too much. We get along, give each other space when we need it."

"Yeah, but to share a room with your sister?" Ryder sat down on the edge of the bed and Andrew just shrugged again.

"It's a tight fit, that's all. Although lately she has been pissing me off about college."

"Why? What's going on now?"

"We got letters from some of the scouts that were at the game. Two offers for each of us, but one of them I don't like, and that's the one school that offered a scholarship to both of us. Of course Andrea thinks we're both going there."

"But?" Ryder asked.

"But I don't want to go there and she just doesn't get it."

Silence settled over them as Andrew flopped over to lie on his bed. He stared at Andrea's side of the room. He should be able to just tell her no. Twins or not, it was his life to live, not hers. "I shouldn't let Andy dictate my life."

"How did you both wind up with the nickname Andy?" Ryder asked.

Andrew reached up and smoothed his hair. "My grandfather, mom's dad, gets confused sometimes. He's really bad with names. When we were younger, like you already heard, we looked a lot alike. So he just shortened it to Andy for both of us and, when he called, we'd both come running. It kind of stuck."

Ryder nodded as if it made sense. "Have the two of you always been close?"

"Of course. We always did everything together growing up. When Mom and Dad signed us up for sports when we were seven, we both decided on soccer. And we've stayed with it."

The room started to warm up to a comfortable temperature. Beneath them they could hear the football game on the television and the cursing and laughter of the men. The doorbell rang and Andrea's laughter rose above the din. Seconds later footsteps thundered up the steps and the door flung open.

"Oh, you're in here."

"Hi, Ryder. Happy Thanksgiving," Sarah said, peering in over Andrea's shoulder.

"You too, Sarah," Ryder replied.

Sarah giggled as she pushed past Andrea into the room, cleared off a spot on the bed, and sat down. Ryder gave her an awkward smile.

"Okay, I admit it's a really tight fit when there're more people in here," Andrew said and frowned. He pushed himself off the bed and grabbed his jacket.

"Where are you going?" Andrea asked, picking something off of her dresser.

"For a walk? Come on, Ryder."

"Wait, Andrew. Charlie called a little earlier. He said he would be by soon to watch the game."

Andrew turned on his sister and frowned. "Why didn't you tell me when he called? I don't know why he's coming over to watch it. He knows I hate football."

She shrugged and flopped down on the floor, leaning back against her bed. "So what? I didn't think it would matter. Besides, I didn't know Ryder was coming over."

"Hey, it's cool. I can watch the game," Ryder said. He looked at Andrew and shrugged.

"No, it's okay. Let's just go."

The two of them left the room and headed downstairs, pulling on their jackets. At the door they slipped on their boots. The open door admitted a blast of cold air, and Andrew took a deep breath as he stepped outside with Ryder. To fend off the cold, they instantly wrapped their arms around themselves.

"Okay, maybe this is torture," Andrew admitted. They started walking.

"Hey, we can always go back to my place. No one's there," Ryder suggested, not looking at him. "And it's warm."

"Yeah, but if Charlie comes over…"

"No offense, Andy, but Charlie's a real prick. He acts like you can only be friends with him, like you're still in third grade or something. I'd say he wanted you if I didn't know how much he was into Sarah."

"Hey, that's not funny!" Andrew gave him a light shove and stepped off the porch onto the frozen ground. "He's just…I don't know. You're new, and he and I have known each other forever. He's a little cautious when it comes to new people."

"Yeah, fine, but no one else has treated me like he has," Ryder pointed out, and shoved his hands deep in his pockets.

"You also only really try to hang out with us," Andrew countered, and headed up the hill behind the house. "I haven't seen you try to hang around anyone else at school or on the weekends."

Ryder trailed after him. "You're not with me all the time, Andy. I've talked to other people. Karina's a nice girl. Just because I only hang out with you outside of school doesn't mean I don't talk to others."

Andrew wasn't sure why, but the admission made him feel uncomfortable. Not much, but enough to feel it.

"We could go to the movies," Ryder suggested after a few minutes, letting the subject of Charlie drop. "We used to do that in Texas. After we had our turkey, we'd drive into San Antonio for the day and catch a movie."

"Who goes to see a movie on Thanksgiving?"

"A lot of people. You should see how busy the theaters get."

"Not here."

"You might be surprised."

"I'll think about it," Andrew said after a few moments.

Up on the hill not a single sound reached them. No loud football game blared on the television, no fans cheered or booed, no girls giggled. Just the two of them, with the old barn standing sentry. The water in the pond had frozen on the edges, but the center remained clear. They stood on the banks. A gust of wind blew and the tree house creaked. Andrew looked up at it, inspecting the rotting boards.

"That's going to fall soon."

Ryder looked up with him, making a small noise. "Never know. Sometimes old things hang on longer than you'd expect."

"Maybe. Andrea and I used to play in it all the time when we were kids. Dad helped us build it one summer. We both used to fit in there so well," he said, a bit wistfully.

Clearing off a spot on a rock, Andrew sat down. He winced and shifted, the natural seat colder than he expected it to be. Ryder sat next to him and together they looked down the hill toward the house. With the leaves off the trees, Andrew could see all the way to the road. Every so often a car drove by, the sound muffled by the distance and the snow blanketing the ground. Ryder moved closer and their shoulders and legs pressed together, giving each other a little extra heat with their shared warmth.

"You know," Ryder started, pausing for a moment. "I like it up here. Despite it being so damn cold all the time, it's nice."

"Do you miss Texas?"

"The warmth, yeah. But this is good, too. I miss some of my old friends, but I guess they weren't really friends."

"Why do you say that?"

"They don't return my calls."

"Oh." Andrew jostled his shoulder against Ryder. "I'm sorry."

"Nah, don't be. I kind of figured they wouldn't. Besides, I've got the best friend I've ever had," Ryder said, giving him a little nudge back.

Andrew smiled. "Do you miss your parents?"

Ryder hesitated before answering. "Yeah. It was hard at first, and it still is sometimes. I miss Mom's cooking. She made the best damn fried chicken ever. And I miss riding with Dad. I wish he hadn't gone, but I know it's what he loves doing, and it's not as if he had a choice."

"I can't imagine what it would be like if my dad went off. I don't know what Mom would do, either."

"It's a hard decision. But with two of you, I think your mom would stay here, don't you?"

"Yeah. Maybe," Andrew paused, and then looked up at him. "Okay, it's cold. Let's go see a movie."

"Really?" Ryder's face lightened and broke into a lopsided grin.

"Yeah, really."

"It's a date," he laughed, pulling Andrew close.

Andrew flushed faintly and nodded. "Okay, a date then. But no food," he warned.

"Oh come on, you have to have some snacks. Popcorn? Soda? Sno-caps?"

"After everything I ate?" Andrew made a face. "You can have it. I'll just watch the movie."

Ryder laughed and pulled him close, pressing a small kiss to his lips before pulling away. Andrew's face stung, but he wasn't sure if it came from the frigid air or the kiss. He pulled Ryder back to give a longer one, deepening it when a small groan emerged from Ryder's throat.

"Let's get out of here and go before Charlie shows up," Ryder said softly when they broke apart. "But don't think you can't repeat that. Anytime."

Chapter Eleven

There were a few more cars in front of the house when Andrew and Ryder returned from the movies in Utica. Ryder had been right and gloated about it; the parking lot of the theater had been full. They bought their tickets to a new action movie that promised to be loud and explosive, bought some snacks—the smell had enticed Andrew, despite his claim of being too full—and found seats. They talked about the movie as they left the theater and headed for home.

Andrew parked in the road to avoid blocking anyone from leaving, and they climbed out of the truck and joked their way up to the front door. It opened as soon as they reached it, and Andrew found himself staring Charlie in the face. "Hey, Charlie."

"I've been here for hours, where the hell did you go?"

"We went to the movies," Andrew said, hesitating only a second. He glanced up at Ryder, who stood there as if bored, hands deep in his pockets. His face was blank.

"Who the hell goes to the movies on Thanksgiving?" Charlie asked, snorting.

"Apparently a lot of people. The theater was nearly full. You should have seen it," Andrew said. He moved past Charlie and stepped inside the house. A new football game must have been on, because the guests still cheered from the other room. Andrew hung his jacket on the coat rack instead of bringing it up to his room, and Ryder put his over it to save room.

"Come watch the game," Charlie said, a hint of anger tingeing his voice. Andrew walked into the dining room and found the table set up with the desserts from before. He looked at them longingly. That pecan pie looked really good, and he didn't usually like pecans.

"Man, you know I hate football."

"Come on, it's the *least* you could do after ditching me here."

"Ditch you? You weren't even here when we left!"

Charlie crossed his arms and leaned against the wall. "Your sister told you I was coming."

"Yeah, after we made plans," Andrew lied. "And she said you *might* be coming. But fine, I'll watch the damn game with you."

Charlie nodded and shot Ryder a dark look before disappearing into the living room. Ryder stared after him. "Man, I don't get it. He really does hate me."

"Don't let it get to you. He's being an ass."

"The rest of the soccer team?" Ryder asked.

"They've got their own groups too, you know?" Andrew shrugged and poured himself and Ryder a cup of soda. "I'll talk to him about it tomorrow. I'll hang out with him and he'll forget this whole thing."

"All right," Ryder said, taking his cup and bumping Andrew with his hip. "Whatever you say. I'll play nice." He winked at him and walked out to the living room, Andrew close behind.

❖

Charlie's room was just as much a disaster as it had been the last time Andrew visited, if not a little worse. He had to wade through junk to get to the desk, and when he pulled the chair out, a pile of papers slipped onto the floor. Frowning, he pushed them off and sat down; the bed was a mess of sheets and clothes.

"How can you live in this mess?"

"What's wrong with it? I know where everything is."

"I'm surprised you haven't had Hazmat come in and designate this hazardous waste or something."

Charlie shrugged and flopped back on his bed, squishing any clean and dirty clothes that were in the way.

Andrew picked a shirt up off the floor, crumpled it into a ball, and tossed it at him.

The two of them never could sit still without talking for long; Charlie didn't like things to be quiet. Andrew thought about that as they sat there awkwardly and wondered what that meant. He and Ryder could sit and not say anything for long periods of time and it felt right. As the minutes passed, he started to squirm uneasily in his seat.

"Man, we always had something to talk about, and we don't anymore."

"To be honest, we never really talked about much," Andrew said. He pushed at a glass on the desk and saw a water mark under it. Inside a sticky residue stained the bottom of the glass a dark brown. He wrinkled his nose in disgust.

"No, but we could talk. Now we can't, because you only hang out with Ryder."

"Whoa, let's not start this, okay? Why do you have to keep bringing it up? I'm here right now, aren't I?"

Charlie sat up and glared at him. "Well, I'm a little pissed off that you abandoned your friends for this new guy. He's not like us, Andrew."

"What the hell do you mean, friends? Who else is pissed off?"

"Sarah. And Andrea."

Andrew pushed off the chair and moved closer, arms crossed. "That's funny, because Sarah hasn't mentioned anything about it, and when Andrea does, it's just to tell me you're pissed off. My problems with Andrea have nothing to do with Ryder."

"There's something wrong with him, Andy, I know it! Do you know who I saw him talking to a few weeks ago? Joshua. Joshua Grayson."

"Yeah? So what if he talked to him. He's got a right to talk to anyone he wants to," Andrew countered. He had a bad feeling about this Joshua talk.

"Come on, you know Josh. Besides, I saw them. And they

looked like they were more than a little friendly, if you know what I mean."

"What are you getting at, Charlie?" It wasn't a question so much as a demand that he just get to the point.

"Josh is a fag. Who else but another fag would talk to him?"

Andrew stared at his friend in disbelief, and he voiced it. "I can't believe you. So what if he talks to Josh. Ryder's a nice guy, and he can talk to whomever he wants. That doesn't make him gay."

"It doesn't make him not gay."

"It doesn't mean anything."

"And you'd know this because?"

"Screw this." Andrew turned for the door and nearly tripped over a pair of jeans. It only made his irritation rise.

"Where are you going?"

"Home. I'm not sitting here listening to you trash him. Like it or not, Charlie, he's my friend. Get over it and grow up. You're acting like you're five years old. Just because Sarah won't give you the time of day doesn't mean you can go around saying shit about the guy she likes."

Charlie leapt off the bed in a flash and grabbed Andrew's arms. He shoved him backward. "Well, why do you think he keeps saying no to her? She's the hottest girl in school. She's throwing herself at him and he says no? That's got to mean something!"

"It means he's not interested. What's so wrong with that? I wouldn't date her either!"

"She's your sister's best friend! Of course you wouldn't date her."

"There are a lot of girls I wouldn't date in school either."

"Yeah, but there are a lot that you *have* dated. Key difference."

Andrew pushed him back to give himself some space. "I don't understand what your problem is, Charlie."

"He hasn't dated *anyone*. Think about it."

"Maybe he has someone back in Texas," Andrew lied.

"Why didn't he mention her?"

"I don't know, and I really don't care. What business is it

of yours? You're not even a real friend to Ryder. Why would he mention his girlfriend to you?"

"Did he mention her to you?"

Andrew saw red. "Man, I can see why Sarah wouldn't want to date you. You're nothing but a selfish jerk."

Charlie had Andrew's arms in a tight grip and shoved him into the wall. "Take it back."

"No. Back off, Charlie." Andrew's voice was low and dangerous, his eyes narrowed, and Charlie just shoved him into the wall again. Something inside Andrew snapped and he gave him a shove right back. Startled, Charlie caught his foot on the same pair of jeans Andrew had tripped over, and he went sprawling, dragging Andrew down with him. They scuffled on the floor, each fighting to gain the upper hand and pin the other to their advantage. Charlie twisted them and ended up on top. Just as he was about to pull his fist back, his mother threw the door open.

"What is going on in here?" she gasped when she saw the two of them on the floor. "Charlie! What has gotten into you? Get off him."

"He started it," Charlie spat as he stood.

"Are you all right, Andrew?"

"I'm fine, Mrs. Wilson. I was just leaving." He stood and shrugged his shirt straight, reaching up to smooth his hair and rub the backs of his knuckles over a spot he knew would be bruised in just a few hours. He gave Charlie a wide berth as he passed through the door and shot him one last glare. He was almost out the door when he heard mother and son arguing. The sounds disappeared as soon as he stepped out the front door and shut it behind him.

❖

"You're back early," Andrew's father said from the kitchen table. He glanced up at him as he walked in and frowned. "What happened?"

"Nothing. Why do you ask?"

"Because you said you were going to Charlie's and come back

an hour later, give or take. Whenever you hang out with him you're gone all day. Did you lie about going to Charlie's?"

"Of course not. I just didn't feel like being there."

"Uh-huh," his father said, setting down a sheaf of papers. "Did you two have a fight?"

Andrew hesitated before pulling out a chair and sprawling in it. "Am I that obvious?"

"The bruise makes it pretty obvious." Dad crossed his arms and sat back. "So what happened?"

"Charlie's just a jerk."

"Is this about Ryder?"

How would he know this had to do with Ryder? Did people see more than he thought? He stopped his train of thoughts, horrified.

What if he knows?

Andrew swallowed. "Charlie doesn't like him very much. He's being ridiculous."

"Why?" his father asked.

"I don't know. Because Sarah likes Ryder and Charlie likes Sarah? But Ryder's turned her down like, four times. So I don't know what he's so worried about."

"I agree with you on that, it is a bit ridiculous." Dad paused, holding his inhale a moment. As he exhaled, he said, "But I can see where he's coming from, too."

Andrew looked up at his father, surprised. "What? How can you agree with him?"

"Don't jump to conclusions, Andy! I said I think I see where he's coming from, not that I agree with him or think he's right. I've noticed you've been hanging around Ryder more, that's all."

"Why shouldn't I? We're friends. He's a better friend than Charlie's been lately."

"I'm not saying you shouldn't. I'm just saying, maybe Charlie feels a little neglected." Dad paused.

Andrew brooded.

"You do a lot with Ryder and don't invite him, and you have been friends with Charlie longer."

"Well, we don't invite him because Charlie wouldn't want to go."

"You sure about that?"

"Well, no, not really. But he said no every time we asked before," Andrew admitted. "So we just stopped asking."

"So, the next time you do something, ask him. It can't hurt to ask. And if he keeps saying no, well then, it's his fault. You'll have made an effort to include him."

Andrew expelled a frustrated sigh. "Thanks, Dad."

His father smiled. "You're welcome. Oh, and Ryder called right after you left. I told him you went to Charlie's already and probably wouldn't be back until later tonight."

"I'll call him in a bit."

Andrew headed upstairs to his room and found Andrea sitting at her desk looking over the letters. Four of them were in front of her, and he had a feeling he knew what they were. With a sigh he sank onto his bed.

"I think we should call UConn, once and for all. We both get a scholarship and they're a Division One school. It's perfect."

"UConn? Connecticut."

Andrea snorted and turned to look at him. "Uh, duh, of course it's Connecticut, idiot. The Huskies, remember? Basketball? They're huge? They have a great soccer team, too, which you should already know."

Andrew reached down and grabbed a magazine from his floor, ready to flip through it, but it was one that Sarah had left behind. "I don't know, though. I kind of wanted to stay close to home."

"Connecticut is close to home. It's only a few hours away. We can come home on weekends if you really wanted to, but we'd get to live on campus. They have a great program, Andrew."

"I was thinking more local," he admitted, finally looking at her. "Local like…maybe Utica or something."

Andrea snorted. "I'd much rather play for UConn. Besides, we haven't gotten offers from Utica."

He didn't care about scholarship offers. Or soccer. "We don't…

have to go to the same school," Andrew replied softly. *She's going to blow up. Any second now*, he thought, slowly counting to himself.

Andrea merely brushed his comment to the side. "Of course we have to. We've agreed to it. We're going to take UConn by storm! The Morris twins. Unstoppable." She grinned at him. "So how do you want to tell Mom and Dad?"

"Andrea, can you just listen? I don't know if I want to go there."

She waved a hand and turned back to her papers, pulling out a pen. "I wonder if anyone else from the team got offers from UConn. It would be cool to room with one of them. But maybe it would be better to room with someone else and get a new experience."

She refused to listen. Scholarship or not, Andrew didn't want to go there. He wanted to stay close to home. He thought about filling out the paperwork for the other college and sending it in without telling her, but that would cause World War III. Andrew sighed and watched Andrea furiously filling in the blanks, signing her soul away to UConn. And, if she had her way, his soul, too.

"If you're worried about filling out the application right, I'll do it for you," she said, distractedly. "Just write your own essay, okay? It's not that hard."

"I don't think that's legal, Andrea."

"It's fine. We have similar handwriting."

"Andrea. You're not listening to me. I don't want to go to UConn."

His sister slowly turned toward him. "You don't know what's best for your future, Andrew. Hello, full scholarships. We'll get to play on the teams. It's a great school with a great soccer program."

Andrew pushed himself off the bed and paced around the small floor space. "I don't want to play soccer forever, Andy. It's just a game. I'll get an academic scholarship for Utica College. I'd like to go there. They have some great academic programs."

"You would rather be a moose than a husky?"

"Yes," Andrew said, steeling himself.

Andrea's eyes narrowed. "You'd settle for a Division Three

school when you were offered to play for Division One? I can't believe you."

"Believe it, Andrea. I don't even know if I want to play."

"That's ridiculous. You'll change your mind. We're going to UConn," she said, her tone sharpening.

Andrew hardened his own words. "You might be, but I'm not."

Andrea turned back to the desk, ignoring Andrew no matter what he said. "We're going to UConn."

Andrew didn't bother replying. It just didn't matter.

CHAPTER TWELVE

The first day back to school after Thanksgiving break always seemed to drag on. The half-year courses were ramping up for finals in a few weeks, and the full-year courses were getting ready for midterms. Teachers were generally stressed about preparing for the exams and were bogged down with work. Students had projects that were coming up or due and were rushing to get them finished. But a bit of festive air still lingered as students talked about the holiday that just passed, or the holiday coming up.

In history that morning, before the bell rang, Sarah sat chatting with Andrew and Ryder about what she had done the day after Thanksgiving. She explained all the amazing deals she had gotten from her shopping trip on Black Friday and bragged about being almost done with shopping for presents.

"I had a little more money this year than I did last, so I bought some things for my friends," she hinted, smiling sweetly at them.

"Who do those friends include?" Andrew asked, cautious. He hated when someone bought him a gift and he didn't get that person anything in return. It made him feel cheap.

"Oh, you know, Andrea, you, Charlie, Ryder."

"Sarah, you really shouldn't have."

"But I found the perfect thing for you, Andy! You'll love it. Trust me!"

Andrew groaned and shook his head while Ryder grinned.

"What are you getting your parents, Ryder?"

"I don't know. There's not much they'd really want, and they're over in Germany, so it'll be difficult to ship it if it's too big."

"Couldn't you buy it online and just have it shipped from the website? It would probably save you money."

Ryder shrugged. "I could look into it I guess. I'll see if there are any new books my mom wants. Those would be pretty hard to buy over there, and shipping online shouldn't be too expensive. I don't know about my dad, though. He's always been tough to shop for."

Sarah was about to pass her question on to Andrew when Mrs. Appleby walked in and motioned for them to take their seats. While she explained the new group project, Andrew's thoughts wandered. Should he get something for Ryder for Christmas? Of course he should. They were dating. How long had they been dating? He counted back on his fingers, eyes widening briefly. It had been nearly three weeks.

Just three weeks? It feels like months.

Andrew pulled out his notebook and a pen. He'd never dated anyone around a holiday, thus freeing him from obligations of buying gifts for a girlfriend, but he didn't think that would be the case this year.

He was still going strong with Ryder, and not sick of him at all. He was having a good time, and he thought Ryder was, too. But what would Ryder want for Christmas? It would only be a month into their relationship, so Andrew didn't want to get anything too big. But it couldn't be too small or stupid, either. It had to be something meaningful, something Ryder would really like.

I can't believe I'm dating a guy.

He couldn't quite believe it was working far better than it had dating Cynthia and Danielle, or any of the other girls. Why hadn't he seen it before?

He didn't notice when class ended and continued to stare at his notes until he felt a hand drop down on his shoulder. He looked up to see Ryder gazing down at him. "Penny for your thoughts?"

"They're not worth that much," he said, smiling and closing his notebook. He stood and brushed against Ryder. It amazed him how that small contact could send a thrill straight down his spine. Even a small touch from his girlfriends had made him cringe unless he had been the one to initiate it. And even then, he'd had to sort of… tune out.

"I'll see you at lunch?" asked Ryder, heading for the door. Andrew nodded and watched him go before gathering up his books. Karina had been waiting for him at the door and followed him out. Sarah remained at the door, waiting for Andrew. When Ryder rounded the corner, she sighed softly.

"He's so cute…it's a shame."

"What? What's a shame? That he keeps turning you down?" he teased, putting it as lightly as he could so she wouldn't be hurt or offended.

"You haven't heard? And you two are such good friends," she said, walking toward her next class. Andrew followed her, a thread of worry beginning to wind through his stomach. He dodged the students that filed through the hallway and lingered at their lockers to keep up with her.

"Heard what?"

"I talked to Charlie over break, and apparently he saw Ryder talking to Joshua Grayson."

"Oh for the love of—that doesn't mean anything!"

"No, I know. But Charlie saw them talking, and he said it seemed more like flirting, because Ryder kept touching him and—"

"You've got to be kidding me. I can't believe this," he muttered, throwing a hand in the air and nearly dropping his books in the process. "Don't you get it, Sarah? Charlie is saying that because he likes you, and he's upset that you're paying more attention to Ryder than you are to him!"

"But that's not all!" she cried, grabbing on to his arm. "I talked to Joe, too," she added with a lowered voice. She glanced around at the people passing and pulled him into a quieter corridor. "You know, Joe Anderson, from your team? He said, like, two weeks after Ryder got here, he came on to him."

Andrew paused and looked at her. "You know Joe is a liar. Remember what he said about Josh Grayson? He says stuff to get attention all the time. When did he tell you this? When it supposedly happened or just now, after Charlie had a chance to talk to him?"

Sarah had to think about it and looked at her classroom door, frowning. "He told me this morning, actually."

Andrew pressed his lips into a grim line. "Nothing but lies. I'm getting tired of them," he hissed and headed for class as the warning bell rang. He didn't bother looking back at her. *This time Charlie's shit has gone too far.*

❖

Andrew put his tray down on the table next to Ryder and leaned close to him. "Charlie's starting crap, and he's getting the other guys from the team in on it."

"What kind of crap?" murmured Ryder, keeping his voice low and glancing around the room. Students still filed into the cafeteria doors as they came from their classes.

"They're trying to get everyone to believe you're gay."

Ryder pulled back and looked at him, shocked. "But I am."

Andrew hissed, "Keep your voice down!" He glanced around again and poked at the strange substance on his plate. "I know you are, but do you really want everyone to believe that?"

After a moment's thought, Ryder shrugged. "If they find out, I don't know if I'd deny it. I only kept it quiet in Texas because of my dad, but he's not here now, is he? And I doubt my aunt and uncle would care that much. They're pretty cool." He glanced over at him, face betraying his concern. "Are you afraid they'll connect us?"

"Kind of, yeah," Andrew admitted.

"I'm not going to force you to do anything you don't want to, or force you out, Andy. I like you."

"I know that, and I like you, too," he said, realizing when he said it that like was too simple a word to explain the surge of feelings Ryder brought out in him. But it wasn't the right place to talk about it. He didn't even know if he *could* talk about it. "But I can't…if they start asking me about us, I'm going to deny it. I'm sorry. I'm not ready to be…I mean, I don't even know if I am… you know…"

Ryder looked disappointed for a moment, but shrugged. His lips were turned up in a smile, but his eyes, the way the shine in them disappeared, expressed his true feelings. "I understand. I've been in your place before, and I'm not all that out myself. I don't know what would be harder. Being like this and not being able to talk to anyone about who you like, or being out and having to worry about people like Charlie," he murmured.

Only seconds after he finished talking, Charlie walked up to the table and hesitated. Andrew glared at him and silently went back to his lunch. He hadn't expected him to sit there, after what happened over break. He heard the tray click against the table and the sound of a chair being drawn out. Charlie sat down and started to eat without saying anything. Tension filled the air so thickly it hung nearly visible in the air between them. Andrew wondered if he could suffocate from how thick the air was. Something had to be done to ease it, but what, he didn't know.

The silence at the table was far from companionable, and Ryder shifted in his seat. Eventually, Andrea and Sarah joined them. Andrea looked at her brother and the two guys, then back at Sarah. Her friend shrugged and stared at her food.

"So," Ryder started, clearing his throat. "I was thinking you guys should all come over after school. We can go riding."

Sarah looked up and over at him. "All of us?"

"Yeah, sure! You, Andrea, Charlie. You guys know how to ride, right?"

"Andrea doesn't," Andrew warned, glancing at Charlie. He wondered what Ryder was trying to do.

"I took lessons a few years ago. But it's been a while," Sarah said. "And Charlie knows how to."

"Really? Great! You guys have to come."

Charlie looked up, glanced at Andrew, and then looked back

at Ryder. His face tensed in anger and unease, and then shifted to a blank calm. "Maybe. If I don't have a lot of homework."

"Since when do you care about homework?" snorted Sarah. Everyone laughed at that, and the strain eased noticeably. Andrew wanted to breathe a sigh of relief.

"So you really want us all to come over?" Andrea asked, leaning over the table.

"Of course. You and Andy can drive me home, and Charlie can drive Sarah." Charlie perked up at that idea, his shoulders relaxing. "That wouldn't be a problem, right?"

"No, not at all," Charlie agreed, glancing at Sarah. He smiled and Andrew could see that he had calmed down. Making the suggestion that Sarah ride with Charlie had been genius on Ryder's part.

"You'll have to take me home, though," Sarah warned.

"No problem. I don't mind."

"Okay then! I guess it's settled," Ryder said, clapping his hands.

Lunch after that was full of laughter and teasing. Charlie reverted back to the way Andrew had always known him. When the lunch wave ended, they gathered their things and headed back to class reluctantly, tossing their things in the compactor as they passed it. Charlie waved and agreed to meet them after school by the truck, and dashed off to class. Sarah and Andrea went ahead, talking excitedly, and Andrew held on to Ryder's arm to hold him back a moment.

"You invited Charlie?"

"Yeah, I figured, if I prove I'm not the bad guy he somehow figures me to be, then maybe he'll just leave it alone. Then you won't have to feel so conflicted. I know you do," Ryder said softly. Not a hint of anger could be seen on his face, though. Andrew wondered how Ryder could be so okay with all of this. He knew, in Ryder's place, he'd be angry.

"Smart, that whole thing with Sarah riding with Charlie."

"Part of my brilliant plan. She won't fit in your truck anyway, and if I look like I'm helping set him up with her, how can he stay pissed at me?" He tapped his temple and winked. "I can be smart when I wanna. This Texan ain't as dumb as y'all might think he is."

Andrew rolled his eyes. "Like we would think that. I just hope this plan of yours doesn't backfire," he warned, heading down the other corridor to his class.

"It won't. How could it?"

"Don't even get me started. See you outside."

The rest of the day dragged for Andrew, and he kept glancing at the time. He wanted it to be two o'clock so he could grab his things and run to the parking lot. Part of him was glad he to be riding with everyone else along, to enjoy something as a group like they did before Ryder came, but another part of him was upset that they had to give up their private riding time just to address the unfair rumors. He enjoyed the riding most of all because it was when he got to spend time with Ryder alone. But if it got Charlie off his back and made him leave Ryder alone, then he figured in the end everything would be worth it.

When the bell finally rang, he grabbed his things and sprinted out of class, pushing past the throng of people emerging from classrooms and lingering in the hallway. He switched his things quickly, grabbing random books, and darted out to the parking lot. Andrew made it to his truck first and leaned against it impatiently.

Ryder, Andrea, Sarah, and Charlie strolled out of the school five minutes later, laughing. When they spotted Andrew at the truck, they waved and walked over to him.

"In a hurry?" Ryder teased.

"No, why would you say that?"

"Oh, I don't know, because you're out here before half the student body?" Sarah waved and headed for Charlie's Jetta. "We'll follow you to Ryder's." Charlie waved as well, the grin on his face nearly splitting it in half as he walked over to his car and opened the door with a flourish for Sarah. She thanked him and slipped inside. Once he shut the door, Charlie gave them the thumbs-up and went around to his side.

"Well, he certainly seems happier," Andrea remarked as she climbed into her spot in the middle of the bench seat.

"What do you expect? It's all part of my plan."

"Oh, you have some genius plan? For what?" she asked Ryder.

"To get Sarah and Charlie together so Charlie will stop being a prick."

Andrea punched his arm. "Now, this I've gotta see."

CHAPTER THIRTEEN

A ndrew sat astride Magpie, one hand covering his mouth to hide his mirth as he watched Ryder shove Andrea up onto Oreo's back. Oreo, an Appaloosa stallion, stood patiently as Andrew's sister nearly fell off the other side before managing to get on. Ryder adjusted the stirrups, grinning as he did so.

"Not a word," she warned Andrew as Ryder moved off to Cobalt and swung up easily into the saddle.

Sarah pulled up alongside her on the back of Butterscotch, a palomino mare. "Looking good there, Andrea. Sure you've got it now?"

"Shut up," Andrea hissed, sitting straighter.

"Don't worry, we'll go slow," Ryder said. Andrew laughed at his sister's discomfort and urged his horse into a walk around Oreo and Andrea.

"We might have to walk the horses ourselves for her to keep up," he teased.

"You, knock it off. I know where you sleep. Don't get cocky just because you've done this before."

"When is he not cocky, that's the question," Charlie piped in as he pulled himself up on Clover, one of the boarded horses. The five of them had quickly saddled the horses and gotten ready to take them out after Ryder's uncle agreed to their choices. The horses still needed exercise and with the five of them it would make the work easier. Clover shifted restlessly beneath Charlie, eager to get to the fields. Only Oreo stood still.

"Don't worry, Oreo's a sweetie. He won't do anything unless you tell him to. He's great for a new rider. Even better than Magpie over there."

"It's not the horse I'm worried about," Andrea said. "It's my neck."

"Your neck is fine," stated Ryder, and led them out to the field. Andrew pulled up alongside him and rode, while Andrea stayed between Charlie and Sarah. They kept an eye on her and coached her on how to sit and move with the horse.

Seeing the fence and wanting to show off what he'd learned, Andrew leaned over Magpie's neck, prompting her to break into a canter. He heard Andrea say something behind him, but he took off. He laughed as he made a circuit of the field and came back. "See?" he called out to Andrea. "It's not so hard!"

"Show-off," Andrea muttered.

The five of them spent the next few hours riding around the fields, racing each other and having fun. Andrea didn't dare do anything more than walk, so she often sat to the side, watching and calling out encouragement to whoever's side she was on at the moment. The sun started to go down just as they finished and finally made it back to the barn. They groomed the horses and put away the tack, and then they all went inside for cups of coffee, tea, and hot chocolate.

"Fine, I admit it," said Andrea as she sipped at her cocoa. "You've gotten really good. But it's all because of Ryder."

The look on Andrew's face was smug. "Finally, something I can do that you can't."

"You two are way too competitive," Sarah joked. She sat on the small love seat next to Charlie, who had his arm around the back of the chair. He looked pleased with himself. Sarah finished her cup of tea and set it on the table in front of her. "I had a lot of fun, Ryder. Thanks for having us."

"No problem. You guys should come again."

"Definitely," Charlie agreed enthusiastically. Sarah gave him a look, and Andrew thought he saw something affectionate in the brief way she looked up at him. But the second she looked back at the group, it disappeared.

"We should probably go, though. I've got homework to finish. You know Ms. Cambridge doesn't care that we just got back from break. She'll give us a pop quiz tomorrow just to prove her point," Sarah pointed out.

"Yeah, she will," Charlie groaned in agreement. "I didn't finish *Hamlet*. Did you?"

Sarah nodded. "I did. Do you want to stay a bit after you drop me off? I've got notes you could use."

"Sure! Great!" he said, jumping off the seat and setting down his cup. "Thanks again, Ryder, but I better get her home."

"You kids drive carefully," Ryder drawled in response. He grinned wickedly at Charlie, who stuck up his finger behind Sarah's back once she'd turned away from the room.

"We better get going, too," Andrea suggested, standing up as well. Andrew shot Ryder a brief, wistful look and stood. He debated asking Charlie to take her home but knew that would be met with resistance.

"Yeah, all right."

"See you tomorrow, Ryder."

Ryder waved and they grabbed their things and headed out to their vehicles. As soon as Andrew climbed in the driver's seat and put his books down next to him, he swore and started shifting through the stack of books, then his bag.

"Wait here a sec, I'll be right back. I forgot something inside."

Andrea huffed and started the truck to warm it up, but waited while her brother ran inside. Ryder held the door open for him and then shut it once he was inside.

"Forgetting something?"

"Yeah, my history book," Andrew said, looking around where their bags had been.

"You didn't take anything out of your bag, and it wasn't in the stack. I don't think you had it with you," Ryder said, and pulled him close. Andrew frowned but stretched up to kiss him.

"Are you sure? It's not in my bag."

"I'm sure. Maybe you forgot it in your locker?"

Andrew winced. "We have homework due tomorrow, too."

"Does Andrea have her book?"

"No, she leaves that one at school and uses mine."

"Well then, come get me early tomorrow and you can copy my homework."

"Really? You're a lifesaver. Thanks!" Andrew sighed in relief.

"Under one condition," Ryder said. Andrew raised an eyebrow and stared at him. "You have to kiss me."

"At school? Ryder—"

"No, idiot. Right now." Ryder rolled his eyes, amused, and slipped his arms around his waist. Andrew responded naturally, his own arms settling across his shoulders for a moment as they kissed. He pulled away and tried to step back, but Ryder held him in place.

"Ryder, I gotta go. My sister's going to come in—" He broke off as Ryder's lips met the skin on his neck and brushed soft kisses there. He shivered and shoved him away, a little uncomfortable with his body's instantaneous reaction. "I've gotta go," he repeated. He didn't give him more time as he bolted from the house and climbed into the truck.

"What's wrong?" Andrea asked. "Where's the book?"

"I left it at school."

"We had homework, Andy!"

"I know! Ryder said we could borrow his tomorrow if we pick him up early." He glanced back at the house and saw Ryder in the window as he backed down the driveway.

"Great. What would you do without Ryder?"

Andrew was beginning to wonder the same thing.

CHAPTER FOURTEEN

With Christmas just around the corner, students crammed for tests and tried to finish projects before the break. Every day after school, Andrew, along with his sister and their two friends, went to Ryder's place to study. Sarah and Charlie had been spending time together without the presence of their mutual friends, and when Charlie asked her to the Winter Semi-Formal, she said yes. When Sarah relayed the information to Andrea, she added that he'd asked her to dinner before the dance and she'd said yes to that as well.

It was finally official. They were dating.

Andrew couldn't have been happier. His best friend wasn't harassing his new friend—no, boyfriend—anymore. He had no reason to. As for his relationship with Ryder, they'd been officially, exclusively—if secretly—dating for over a month. For their first-month anniversary, which Ryder insisted on celebrating even though Andrew felt foolish, they went to a movie and had dinner at a modest, family-owned restaurant just outside of town. Even though they couldn't do anything as audacious as hold hands in the bright restaurant, they both felt happy and that was enough.

Sometimes Andrew wondered what it would be like if he told his sister. How would she react if she knew about him? How would his parents react? Or Gram and Pop? At least he knew Andrea treated Josh Grayson well enough, and he was the one student in their school who everyone knew was gay. Though he'd never admitted it, he'd also never denied it. Maybe Andrew could tell Josh. Maybe Josh wouldn't tell anyone, Andrew thought…and then changed his mind instantly. No. Not until he knew for sure Josh was gay. Andrew had never treated Josh poorly, but it's not like he helped him either. Josh could use the information against him, and Andrew wasn't willing to risk it.

The Winter Semi-Formal took place the Saturday before Christmas vacation. The cafeteria had already been decorated for it, and students were getting excited. Nearly the entire student body bought tickets. Andrea had gotten a date with Michael, one of the soccer players from Andrew's team. Ryder had talked to Andrew about going to the dance, but Andrew flat-out refused to go with him. That wasn't something he could do, and, after his initial disappointment, Ryder agreed. But he still wanted to go, so they found their own dates and agreed to meet at a restaurant before.

Ryder had his pick of girls but settled on a quiet junior, Melissa Jenkins. He had met her in art class, and she had thin-framed glasses that sat on a button nose and hid hazel eyes. Her mousy brown hair hung straight to her shoulders. Overall, she was pretty cute, Andrew figured, though he'd had a difficult time deciding which girls were cute and which weren't since he had started dating Ryder. No one registered on his radar anymore.

Andrew's date was another senior, Karina Hill, from the girl's track team and his first-period history class. He'd known her since the sixth grade and thought she would be fun. She agreed to go with him when he said he would drive.

Of course, they couldn't go looking like slobs, so Andrew and Ryder went shopping in Utica the night before the dance.

"What do you think? Khakis or black pants?"

Ryder frowned at the choices Andrew held up. "Black, I think. It's a semi, right? The khakis are kind of too dressed down. Go with the black."

"All right, fine. What color shirt, oh master of fashion?"

Ryder handed him a bright blue button-down. "This. It'll make your eyes pop."

"Do I have to wear a tie?"

"Absolutely."

Andrew glared at him and waited for him to settle on a different style of pants with an emerald green shirt. Held up against him, his eyes nearly glowed.

"Hey, just who are you trying to win over?" murmured Andrew, looking around to make sure they were alone.

"Oh, I don't think I need to win anyone over. I've got you."

Flushing, Andrew quickly walked away from him to look at the different ties. He finally settled on a darker blue that went well with the shirt. Ryder grabbed one as well and they went to pay.

Before they went home they decided to make a detour to grab something to eat. The Roadside Diner was nearly deserted so they stopped there for a quick bite. Looking like a large can tipped on its side, the outside had been repainted recently and shone a bright red beneath the gleaming metal of the roof. Booths lined the wall facing the street, affording patrons a view of the road and parking lot. Along the other wall stood a long counter with stools spaced every two feet for single diners, and the grills in plain sight so everyone could watch their orders being made. A tall man in a white T-shirt and apron stood at the grills, cleaning them off. A cheerful waitress in a bubblegum pink, smock-like dress named Shelly sat them in the booth in the corner that gave them a view on two sides. Once they were seated with a glass of water each, Ryder stretched out, letting his long legs brush against Andrew's.

Andrew felt his face heat and frowned a little, glancing around. "Ryder…"

"Oh come on, no one will see," Ryder argued. "Barely anyone's even here," he added, looking pointedly around. "So is this place any good?" He pulled his legs back a bit, resting just his knees against Andrew.

"Of course. We come here all the time. We just got here before the dinner crowd."

The waitress returned and handed them menus. She took their order for drinks and disappeared to fill them and tend to the rest of the patrons while they browsed the menu.

"So," Andrew started after a long pause. He set his menu

down, having decided on the classic burger and curly fries. "Are you excited about the dance?"

"As excited as I can be for going with some girl I don't know and don't like."

"She seems nice enough."

"Yeah, she really is. I mean I like her, but I don't...*like* her. I don't want her like that. I just hope she doesn't think that's what this is about. I tried to make it clear."

"She seems really quiet. I don't think it'll be a problem."

Ryder shrugged. "Nah, you're probably right. What about you?"

"What about me?"

He looked up from his menu. "Are you excited?"

Andrew thought about it and shrugged as well. "Yeah, I guess I am. I always liked the dances before; don't see why this would be any different. It'll just be weird, you know?"

"How so?"

"Well..." He hesitated and fidgeted with the edge of the menu. "I was always dating the person I went with before, and we would leave early together. Go back to her place, usually. Or somewhere."

Ryder watched him, the look in his eyes far from innocent. "Well, we could always leave the dance early and go back to my place."

Andrew scowled, though the suggestion did intrigue him. Shelly approached and set down their glasses of soda. "What'll it be, boys?"

"Classic burger with curly fries."

"And I'll have a cheeseburger with sweet potato fries," Ryder added.

"Sure thing, be ready in ten."

Shelly took the menus and disappeared behind the counter. The boys leaned a little closer to talk.

"Do you want to?"

"Want to what?" Andrew asked, feigning ignorance while knowing very well what Ryder wanted. He looked down at the Formica tabletop and scratched at a water mark on it.

"Come back to my place after the dance."

"I don't know, Ryder. I mean, your aunt and uncle will be there."

"So?"

"And that'll just look weird if I go back to your place afterward. I don't know," Andrew said. He shifted in his seat and glanced around again. For the first time he noticed a small group of students from school sitting on the far side of the diner. He didn't know their names but recognized them from the hallway. One of the boys, a sophomore, he thought, looked over and nodded, giving him a small wave. Andrew returned the gesture.

Ryder probably figured by the uncomfortable silence that Andrew was not ready for this topic because he steered it back to safer ground, which Andrew was grateful for. Maybe once they were alone, he'd be able to open up more. "What are you doing over Christmas break?"

"On Christmas Eve we always visit my dad's parents in Buffalo. We have dinner there and open the gifts from that side of the family. Then on Christmas Day my mother's parents come down to spend the day with us. It's pretty quiet, but it's fun. There's a lot of food, but not as much as at Thanksgiving."

"That was a lot of food."

"Always is."

"So, what else."

"Let's see…after we open presents and eat, we watch movies all day. Old Christmas movies and some newer ones. And if there's snow on the ground, we go sledding at the hill down the road."

"Sledding?"

"Yeah." Andrew laughed. "You're probably thinking that we're too old for that, huh? But I swear it's a blast. Sometimes Charlie and Sarah come out with us if they can't deal with their families anymore. But it's great when it's just the six of us. My grandfather tries to steer his sled to run us over. He acts like he's five years old."

They enjoyed a moment of laughter and Ryder leaned forward

on an elbow, chin propped up in his hand. "Sounds like a lot of fun."

"Yeah. What are you going to do? Did you hear from your parents yet?"

"They said hello, but they're going to be busy over there, I guess. I'm not sure what my aunt and uncle are doing. I think they usually go to my aunt's family farther upstate, but I don't really know any of them. It'll be weird, I think. But I don't want to keep them from going just because of me."

"You might have fun. Maybe there's someone your age?"

"No way. All the kids in the family are way younger. I'm talking like ten years between the oldest and me. And my aunt said they have this tradition, that if you're a married couple, you sit at the 'adult' table, and if not, even if you bring a date, you're still a kid and sit at the 'kid' table. Which means I'll be stuck with God knows how many screaming brats." He affected a shudder, which got a small chuckle out of Andrew.

"Sounds horrible."

"It does, doesn't it?"

They broke off the conversation when the waitress arrived with their plates of food and set them down on the table. "If you boys need anything, you just call me over."

"Thanks," they said in unison.

They dug into their meals and ate quietly for a few minutes. Andrew stole some of Ryder's sweet potato fries, and in retaliation, he stole some of Andrew's curly fries. They both worked through their meals quickly.

"You're right, this place is good," Ryder agreed around a mouthful of his cheeseburger.

"Told you." Andrew set his burger down and picked up an extra-tightly-curled fry and started to play with it, stretching it like a slinky. "Maybe you could come spend Christmas at my place," he finally offered, studying the fry intensely.

Ryder's mouth was full of fries so it took him a moment to answer. "You mean that? Thanks, Andy, but I don't know how your parents would take it. I mean, you have your own traditions and stuff, you know? Wouldn't want to ruin that."

"I can still ask."

"Don't worry about it."

"I'm going to anyway," Andrew argued, and finished the fry he'd unsuccessfully stretched out. Ryder glared at him a little before finishing his food. Andrew took a little longer. They sat and finished their drinks before paying and leaving their waitress a tip. She smiled and waved as they left, inviting them to come back soon.

"You know," Ryder said thoughtfully as he climbed into the passenger side of Andrew's truck, "I really would love to spend our first Christmas together. I mean, I would understand if your parents said no, but it would be nice to spend the day with you."

Andrew glanced over at him as he turned the key in the ignition. *First Christmas.* He'd never had a first Christmas with anyone. He'd never had a first holiday with anyone. He smiled to himself as he backed out of the space. *If we have a first Christmas, are we going to have another first holiday?*

CHAPTER FIFTEEN

Andrew arrived at the dance with Karina at seven thirty. He had picked her up at six and headed to the Italian restaurant in the center of town and met everyone else there. It seemed like half the school population decided to go there before the dance because hardly any seats remained open. They couldn't find ten seats together, but they were close enough that they could lean over and talk without interrupting too many people around them. Even then, half the time the other tables got into their conversations anyway. Relief flowed through Andrew when they all got up to leave for the dance.

Karina looked beautiful in her knee-length, cream-colored dress. Held up with three thin straps on each shoulder, it went well with her darker skin. She'd pulled her hair up high on her head and a few curls escaped to frame her face. She was thin and tall, nearly his height, and most of it leg. Holding out his arm like a gentleman, he gave her a goofy grin and led her into the dance. She laughed and shook her head.

"I'm glad I said yes. I would be missing a hell of a party," she said, and Andrew agreed.

Though the cafeteria had been decorated before, it looked completely different without the harsh white lights on. The long tables had been packed away, and only a few of the round ones remained around the edges of the dance floor. Against the wall were chairs for students to sit on when they decided they'd had enough dancing. A strobe light reflected above the DJ, throwing bright patterns on the floor. The snowflake motif repeated in cut-outs and banners around the room. A few groups of chaperones were huddled here and there around the floor, keeping a close eye on the students.

An arm wrapped around Andrew's shoulder and he looked up to see Ryder grinning widely. "So this is how y'all party up here, eh?"

Melissa stood next to him in a simple black dress that went just past her knees. It had a small sash around the waist that tied in a bow at the back. She looked around a bit nervously, with Ryder's other arm secure around her waist. Andrew noticed she wasn't wearing her glasses.

"Contacts?" he asked, and she blinked up at him in surprise.

"Oh, yes," she said so softly Andrew had to strain to hear her.

"I love your dress," Karina said with a gentle smile. Melissa returned it and they moved off to the side to talk to each other.

"Guess they know each other," said Ryder with a shrug. Andrew nodded.

The music changed and soon the girls dragged them onto the dance floor. Andrea and her date, along with Charlie and Sarah, popped up next to them seconds later. They all moved to the music, their bodies close and swaying together with the beat. Melissa's discomfort faded quickly with Ryder, and she livened up, wrapping her arms around his shoulders and letting him rest his hands at her waist or on the small of her back. Karina and Andrew danced apart for a while, until she turned, fitting her back against his chest. Because of Andrew and Karina's nearly identical height, the girls traded partners, eliminating the awkward difference.

"Maybe I should have come with Ryder," Karina teased. "You short boys are seriously lacking."

"I'm wounded," Andrew replied jokingly, holding on only tighter to Melissa, who visibly blushed even in the low lights.

The four of them danced through three more songs with a techno beat, the girls dancing between the boys. Every so often Andrew caught Ryder's gaze and held it. Ryder's eyes were heated, but he continued to dance, entrancing Andrew even more. His movements were fluid, just like when he rode Cobalt. *I wonder where else he can move like that*, Andrew wondered and had to stop that train of thought quickly. Even though he was starting to sweat from the heat in the room, his face flushed for other reasons.

When the music turned slow, the girls switched back to their original dates and danced with them. As Andrew moved in a slow circle with Karina, his hands secure around her waist, he caught a glimpse of Ryder watching him. As their eyes met, his expression turned serious once again, almost burning through him. Andrew held his stare when the song ended. With a barely perceptible movement, Ryder nodded toward the door. Andrew flicked his eyes over to confirm it and stepped away from Karina.

"Where you going?" she asked.

"I'll be back in a few. I've gotta get some air." He reached up to wipe his sweaty forehead and she wrinkled her nose. She and Melissa were soon lost in the crowd when he stepped toward the doors leading into the school hallways.

Andrew and Ryder waved to the teacher standing watch at the door and slipped off down the hall. They could still hear the music, and it echoed in the dark, empty corridors. When they reached the end, Ryder grabbed him and pulled him into the shadows, pushed him against the wall and kissed him hard. Andrew returned the kiss just as eagerly, forgetting for the moment that they were in the school and just a few feet away were all their friends and classmates.

When Ryder pulled back, Andrew struggled to catch his breath. At some point during the kiss, his arms had wrapped around Ryder's shoulders and pulled him closer, and Ryder's arms were slipped around his waist.

"We have to go back before they miss us," Andrew whispered between kisses.

"I know." Leaning close to Andrew's ear, Ryder whispered, "Come back to my place tonight."

Andrew reached up and brushed a hand against his forehead, brushing away a droplet of sweat and nodded. His heart pounded and blood raced through his body, making it hard for him to think clearly. *Back to Ryder's place tonight.* Images flashed through his mind, none staying long enough for him to grasp fully, but the intent in them was clear enough. Andrew found it suddenly harder to breathe and his palms tingled. His closed his fingers, making a tight fist to dig his nails into his sensitive skin and fight off the sensation. Ryder must have noticed because his lips suddenly quirked up in a smile. Those green eyes caught the little light there was and reflected back at Andrew.

Before Ryder could say anything more, Andrew pulled him back for another kiss, pushed him away, then hurried back toward the cafeteria.

❖

Karina saw Andrew and waved him over, holding a bottle of water out to him. "Here. I got you water. You look like you could use it."

"Thanks," he said as he snagged the bottle and took a deep drink from it. He loosened his tie and unbuttoned half his shirt to help cool off. Karina nudged him and pointed.

"Looks like Sarah and Charlie are getting along just fine now."

He followed her finger and nodded. "They always got along fine before anyway." He shrugged. The pair stood off in the corner, arms and lips locked on each other.

"Not like that."

"No, not like that."

The dance ended at eleven, and the students lingered in the parking lot by their cars. Despite the cold air, they were without their jackets; they were still sweating from all the packed bodies dancing in the enclosed space. Andrew leaned up against his truck where he had parked it next to Ryder's borrowed car.

"So what are we doing? Going to the diner?" Charlie asked.

"Are you nuts? It'll be packed," Andrew said.

"Well, I've gotta get Melissa home, so I'm out," Ryder added.

"And I have a family thing tomorrow morning," said Karina, making a face. "Can you take me home, Andy?"

"Sure."

"After you drop her off stop by my place, Andy," Ryder said, waving as he opened the door for Melissa.

Andrew nodded, trying to act cool though his heart raced. "You set for your ride, Andrea?"

"Yeah, Michael's going to take me home," Andrea replied with a wink. She held a finger up to her lips and Andrew nodded. Of course he wouldn't tell. She stretched and waved to everyone else. Michael waited at his car for her and climbed in as soon as she started toward him.

Andrew slid into the cab next to Karina, tossed the tie between them, and backed out of the parking spot to join the line of cars waiting to leave. Next to him, Karina stayed silent and watched the people passing by the truck. She waved a few times to some of her friends as they passed.

"Thanks for inviting me, Andy. I had a great time," she said after they pulled out of the lot and turned toward her side of town.

"Me too," he admitted, smiling. He turned the heat on as soon as the truck had warmed, and they stopped shivering seconds later when the hot air hit them.

"Ahh, that's better."

"That's the one really shitty thing about this truck. That and the radio, or so Ryder says."

Karina laughed and pointed out a shortcut down one of the service roads that ran through a farmer's field. "Mr. Jones doesn't mind us using it. He keeps it plowed in the winter. Just as long as we don't go off it or race he says we can keep using it," she said when Andrew hesitated. He turned onto the field and turned his high beams on.

All the lights were off in the house when they pulled up, and no cars were in the driveway. Andrew put the truck in park and waited for Karina to get out, but when she didn't, he figured she was waiting for him to walk her to the door. He reached out to open his door but her hand on his leg stopped him. He glanced over at her and realized how close she had moved toward him.

"Karina?"

"Shh," she whispered and stretched up, giving him a soft kiss. Her lips were smooth and warm against his, different from what he'd grown used to in the past weeks. He pulled back and gently pushed her away. "Come inside with me?"

"Karina, I can't…"

She tilted her head, eyes pinning him with a stare, forcing him to shift uncomfortably.

"It's not that I don't appreciate the offer," he stammered, looking out the window. "It's just—"

"It's Ryder, isn't it?"

"What?" Head snapping around, he turned to look at her and nearly gave himself whiplash in his surprise. He tried to cover his reaction and not panic. "What about Ryder?"

"The reason you won't come inside. I'm right, aren't I?"

Inside, Andrew knew he should deny everything, act like it was nothing, maybe look horrified by what she implied, but he couldn't. He just sat there and stared at her, then looked back out the window.

His silence answered everything. "I figured." She slid across the seat and pushed the door open.

"What made you ask that?"

Karina turned to him and shut the door again, her smile soft and pleasant. He wondered briefly if it was an act and if he'd suffer the consequences later. Her next words proved that wrong.

"You haven't been with anyone in over a month—"

"That doesn't mean anything," Andrew argued.

"I'm not finished. You haven't been with anyone in over a month and you're *never* without a girlfriend. In all the time I've known you, you've bounced around so often it's hard to keep up with you. You're always hanging out with him—"

"I always hang out with Charlie, too."

Karina sighed and leveled a glare at him. "Can I finish, please?"

"Sorry."

"Thank you. There's that, and the way he always has to touch you. The way he looks at you and the way you look at him. I don't think you even realize what you're doing. You're completely unaware of yourself. When you left the dance for a few minutes with him, you came back and acted all jumpy."

"Just from all that you figured it out?"

"It was a hunch, and I see the two of you every day in class. I figured you were different a long time ago, anyway. You never act comfortable with your flavor of the week. I guess you hadn't found what you'd wanted because you were looking in all the wrong places, huh?"

Andrew nodded, staring straight out the windshield. "I guess you're right, but I didn't know. I mean Ryder's the first! I didn't even think…" He trailed off.

She smiled again and patted his arm. "I won't tell anyone, I promise. Don't worry about it. You're not *too* obvious. I only noticed because I have the eyes of a hawk and see everything." She tapped the side of her face for emphasis and scrunched up her eyes and nose.

Andrew chuckled softly and she winked and closed the distance between them again and kissed his cheek.

"Thanks again, Andy."

The car door opened and admitted a blast of cold air. She shivered violently in her jacket and turned back to him one more time. "And don't you dare back out on whatever Ryder offers you tonight just because I know about you two. I'll ask him, and if he says nothing happened, I'll kick your ass." Karina shut the door and made her way to her porch. Once she was inside with the door shut and the lights on, Andrew backed out of the driveway and headed for Ryder's house.

Twice he nearly lost his nerve and turned around to go home, but something Karina had said changed his mind, and he kept on driving. *She knows and she isn't freaked out by it. She knows and I don't feel as bad as I thought I would. And she's not going to tell a single person.* He smiled and pressed his foot a little harder on the gas. He felt good, relieved almost, to have someone know his and Ryder's secret. And though he was nervous about what—if anything—would happen tonight, Ryder waited for him.

CHAPTER SIXTEEN

Ryder had the door open for Andrew before he had to knock. He looked questioningly at the empty driveway and then back at Ryder.

"Aunt Lisa left a note. Some friend of hers from college is in town and she went out with Uncle Kyle to meet up with her. Said they'd be out until one or so, and to make sure I locked everything up before I went to bed."

"That seems too perfect for your plans," muttered Andrew as he pulled off his coat and put it on the rack.

"Okay, so maybe I knew about the friend visiting in advance and that's why I asked you over," Ryder amended, looking far from innocent like the sheepish expression he failed to pull off.

"Sneak." Andrew sat down on the love seat in front of the fire to warm up. Ryder flopped down next to him, slid his arms around his shoulders, and pulled Andrew against him. Andrew let his head fall into place on his shoulder.

Ryder's lips were soon in his hair, pressing light kisses all over. His long fingers worked into the short locks and brushed them back.

"Karina knows about us."

The movement of Ryder's fingers stopped. "Why do you say that?" he asked after a moment's hesitation. His lips were still against Andrew's hair and he felt them move when he talked. It felt kind of nice.

"Because she kissed me, and when I didn't want to go inside with her she flat-out asked if it was because of you."

"You didn't deny it?" asked Ryder, surprise coloring his voice.

"I wanted to. But I couldn't. Besides, she had it figured out. I don't think she would have believed me if I had said no." He paused. "Are you upset? She promised she wouldn't tell anyone," he said, rambling on nervously. His stomach flip-flopped inside.

Ryder's laughter came softly and he shook his head. "No, I'm not upset. Just surprised. And a little relieved. Was she okay with it?"

"Yeah. Seemed it. I think she knows about tonight," he added, keeping what she said to himself.

"You don't want to leave, do you? Because she knows? We don't really have to do anything if you're not comfortable..."

"I'm okay. I don't want to. Leave, I mean. I don't want to leave," he corrected. The warmth of Ryder's arm left his shoulders and he looked up at him. Ryder took his hand and pulled him up.

Their bodies were close, and Andrew felt a small tremor run through his body. Sure, he'd had sex plenty of times, but never with a guy. He felt nervous, but the thought of something new excited him, and his body reacted to it. He couldn't help but feel smug when he realized Ryder's body reacted as well. He'd never been able to tell if his girlfriends really enjoyed being with him or faked it. With Ryder he wouldn't have to question it.

Ryder backed them up toward the stairs, and then turned and walked up with him. Andrew followed, glancing down at the front door briefly. Once in the room, Ryder shut the door behind them and locked it. Just in case.

Before Andrew had time to argue, Ryder had him backing up toward the bed, and when his knees caught on the edge, Andrew toppled over onto it. He yelped in surprise as he fell back.

"Cute," Ryder teased, and dropped onto the bed next to him.

Any protest from Andrew was cut off as their lips met. Ryder's hands slid to his waist and up the back of his shirt and the tee he wore under it. He made a small noise of frustration when his hands got caught up in the material. Moving his hand, he rolled them over and sat up on Andrew's hips. Fingers deftly undid buttons and pushed the shirt open.

Ryder tugged his own shirt over his head and tossed it to the floor. Andrew's eyes raked down his smooth chest, down to his hard stomach and the thin line of hair that trailed down past the waistband of his pants.

"Sit up," Ryder commanded, his voice gone husky. Andrew did and helped pull both of his shirts off. They landed somewhere on the floor near Ryder's.

It was Andrew's turn to be impatient, and he roughly pulled Ryder's face down for a hard, bruising kiss. He shifted and managed to spill Ryder onto the bed beneath him and straddled his hips. His hands ran over his smooth torso, eliciting a small groan from Ryder. Andrew allowed his hands roam toward the belt, but Ryder stopped him. He looked up, blinking in confusion.

"What are you doing?" Ryder demanded.

"What does it look like I'm doing?" replied Andrew, hesitating.

Ryder laughed softly and sat up, pushing his hands away. "I think you've got this backward here."

"But I thought we…aren't we going to have sex?"

"Yes, we are. But you've got it backward."

"Huh?" Andrew let himself be pushed back onto the bed. *What does he mean by that? It can't be that different from sleeping with a girl.*

"We're doing this my way since it's your first time."

Realization dawned on him and Andrew flushed scarlet. He watched as Ryder's hands removed his belt. He watched him, just lying there, excited as before but with a bit of apprehension mingled in.

When Ryder leaned over him and reached into the drawer in the nightstand, he knew what to expect. He'd been down this path before with his girlfriends. He swallowed nervously, heart pounding in his chest, ready to burst. His whole body tensed and he shivered suddenly.

He closed his eyes and felt Ryder above him. When a soft voice encouraged him to open them, he did, though just a crack. Ryder smiled and captured his lips in a gentle kiss.

"Just relax," Ryder murmured against him. "Relax and let go."

CHAPTER SEVENTEEN

Andrew lay in the bed with Ryder, dressed in a pair of his sweatpants. They were too big on him and hung off his slim hips when he stood. Ryder's chest felt warm against his back, and he could feel his steady breathing. The arm draped over his hips twitched every so often and tickled against his skin. He wanted to get out of the bed and stretch, but didn't want to wake Ryder when he did.

He didn't know how much time had passed, but he eventually drifted off to sleep. When he woke again, the sky outside the window had just started to lighten, and the breathing against his back had changed.

"Morning," Ryder murmured, pressing a kiss to the back of his neck. Andrew shivered and closed his eyes.

"Morning."

"How are you feeling?"

Andrew took a few moments to assess how he felt from his position on his side and finally responded, "Fine."

"Really?" Ryder propped himself up and peered over Andrew's shoulder at him. The heat across his face exposed his discomfort. "I think you're a terrible liar." Andrew swatted at him, but Ryder dodged and climbed out of the bed. Andrew kept his focus on the wall and heard the door open and click shut as Ryder left. A minute later he heard water rush through the pipes as the shower started.

Memories from the night before started to surface and he felt the urge to hide under the covers. Pulling them up over his head, he groaned softly.

What the hell do I do now?

He shook his head. They hadn't heard his aunt and uncle come home, but he knew they must have because the delicious fragrance of roasting coffee drifted up to him. He was lured out by it and almost went downstairs to get some when he stopped himself. All it took was one look at the mirror on Ryder's wall and he ducked back, embarrassed.

The coffee could wait until after he showered.

❖

Ryder let him borrow some clothes and he gratefully accepted. They were a little big on him, but his belt kept them from slipping off. He felt much better after the hot shower, and even more so after drinking a cup of coffee.

Ryder's uncle nodded at him from across the table and winked. "I know that look," he teased.

Andrew stared at him, startled, and glanced quickly in Ryder's direction. He didn't seem to have noticed.

"Uh, what?"

"Heavy partying last night? Feeling a little hungover?"

He could have laughed his relief. "Yeah," he said with a small smile. "Just a bit."

"Shouldn't be drinking at your age. Take it easy today. You boys don't have anything planned, do you?"

"Nah, maybe go riding a little later, but that's it."

"Yeah, and I should get home sometime today. At least call my parents and let them know I'm still alive." Andrew laughed. "Who knows if Andrea told them I came over here."

"Actually, they already called," he said through his coffee. "Apparently she didn't."

"Your sister is brilliant, Andy."

Andrew groaned and let his head drop to the table. "Am I in trouble?"

"Didn't sound like it. I told them that you were here. They seemed relieved. Maybe you better call and tell them your sister was supposed to let them know."

"They'll just say I should have called," grumbled Andrew, but he pushed himself up for the phone anyway. He stepped out into the hall to make the call and waited for someone on the other end to pick up.

It was his mother.

"Hey, Mom."

"Andrew! You scared me half to death when you didn't come home last night! I thought you'd gone to Charlie's but he said you weren't there, and—"

"Whoa, Mom! Take it easy! I told Andrea. I thought she was going to tell you."

"Well, she didn't. And you should have called."

"All right. I'm sorry. But I'm fine."

His mother hesitated on the line, and Andrew waited for the question he knew she would ask. "You weren't drinking last night, were you?"

"No," Andrew said, and shook his head though he knew she couldn't see it. "I swear we weren't."

"Okay. I believe what you say."

"Great." Andrew rolled his eyes.

"What time are you coming home?"

"I'm not sure. We might go riding."

"All right. Let me know if I should keep dinner out for you."

"Okay. Oh, and Mom?"

"Yes?"

"Would it…" Andrew hesitated. "Could Ryder spend Christmas with us?"

"What? Why? He has his own family to spend Christmas with."

"But that's the thing. His mom and dad are in Germany, and he's only got his aunt and uncle here. They go to his aunt's family's place up north, and he doesn't know anyone there. There's no one his age on that side of the family. He doesn't really want to go, I talked to him."

His mother sighed. "Andrew…"

"Mom."

"I'll talk to your father and see what he says, and if he's okay with it, then we'll talk to the Kensingtons. But they may want him to go, honey. I know he's your friend, but it's also a big family holiday."

"All right, but you'll ask Dad?"

"When he gets home."

"Thanks."

He hung up the phone, returned to the table, and settled back in his chair. "Everything's cool," he said when Mr. Kensington looked up at him. "No trouble."

"That's good to hear."

❖

Later that day Andrew and Ryder helped Mr. Kensington muck out stalls in the barn. They were working together in Cobalt's stall while the horse stood just outside, tied up. He seemed to be watching them, Andrew thought, wondering what they were doing. After hanging out with Ryder and the horses so much, he realized how expressive and curious they were.

"I asked my mom about Christmas," Andrew said between lifting a pile of dirty hay and dumping it in a wheelbarrow.

"Yeah? What did she say?"

"She said she would talk to Dad. If he's okay with it, they'll talk to your aunt and uncle."

"Man, that's great. Your parents are so cool."

"They haven't agreed yet," warned Andrew.

"I know, I know. But my parents wouldn't even think about it. It would just be flat-out no." Ryder paused to wipe at the sweat on his forehead. "I hope they know I wouldn't be like, leeching off them. I don't want them to think that."

"I'm sure they wouldn't think that. Mom and Dad love you."

"So did you finish Christmas shopping yet?" Ryder asked, changing the subject.

"Of course. I wasn't going on Christmas Eve again this year. I made that mistake last year. I couldn't buy anything because there was nothing left. Dad always goes last minute and drags Andrea. It's kind of funny." Andrew laughed. He didn't mention the gift he had found for Ryder that was currently tucked under his bed where his sister wouldn't be able to find it. "Did you finish?"

Ryder nodded. "Yeah, I went in with my aunt a while ago. Mom and Dad should have gotten their presents by now; I shipped them out two weeks ago. You wouldn't believe how much it cost to ship. It was almost as much as the gifts themselves! But Aunt Lisa helped me pay for it."

"That was nice of her."

"Yeah, definitely."

The two of them tossed some fresh hay into the stall, then moved on to the next one and started to clear it out. Ryder dumped out the bucket of water and put it aside. "What do y'all do for New Year's Eve up here?"

"Go to someone's house and party, usually. Last year everyone went out to Fisher's farm. He graduated last year, so I guess that's out. I don't know. We'll have to see what comes up. Word will get around if there's anything. What did you do in Texas?"

Ryder laughed. "I never went out. I just stayed home with my parents, watched some special, and went to bed."

"Oh. Sounds interesting," Andrew lied.

"Nah, it's okay, you can say it. It was boring as hell," Ryder admitted.

"What do *normal* teenagers do, then?" Andrew smirked.

"The same as up here. There were parties around, though not many in my town. Most went out to one of the bigger towns nearby or into the city for the night."

"Were there fireworks there?"

"Sure, mostly privately owned, though. Nothing the town put

on. On a really clear night you could see the fireworks all the way from the next town. Here?"

"Same. People buy them, mostly the handheld stuff. But on the Fourth of July, the town goes all out. It's great. There are a few places where you can see the show really well. If you're still here then…" Andrew trailed off and stopped raking the hay.

"Andy?" Ryder stopped and looked down at him, a little concerned at the sudden lack of conversation.

"Huh? Oh, sorry."

"What's wrong?"

"Nothing…I just realized you might not be here over the summer, that's all." The thought of that hurt. He wondered what Ryder had planned for college, toyed with the idea that they might end up at the same school. *Or we might not*, he thought as he stared at the ground.

"Hey, I might or I might not be. I haven't decided what I'm doing yet, okay? So let's not think about it. Let's just think like I am going to be here—that way if I am, we'll have stuff to do."

"And what if you're not?"

"Then we'll talk from wherever I am!"

"But what about our plans, then?"

"We'll reschedule them."

Andrew stared at him, upset. "Would you want to come back after you leave?"

Ryder abruptly dropped the shovel he held and crossed the small distance between them. Before Andrew could step back, Ryder had invaded his space, pulling him close, and kissed him until his body relaxed. He pulled away after a few moments and rested his forehead against Andrew's.

"Andrew, look at me. I—"

"Oops! Sorry, boys!" Ryder jumped back and Andrew saw his uncle standing there. Mr. Kensington turned away and strode off quickly.

Andrew stood frozen to his spot, eyes wide and face pale. "D-did he see us?" he eventually whispered.

"I don't know," Ryder whispered back. When he finally moved, he peeked outside of the stall and found his uncle on the other end of the barn, tossing hay into Dante's stall. "Holy shit."

"We're so screwed," Andrew moaned. "He's going to tell my parents and my parents are going to flip out and—"

"Andy, shut up. I don't think it's going to be that bad."

"How do you know that?"

"Because he didn't launch himself at us and kill us right then? I don't know. Let's try to be rational about this. Look, let's just see what he wanted, okay? We don't even know yet if he saw us."

"You go. I can't face him."

"You boys finished so we can talk?" Mr. Kensington called from the other side of the barn, with what sounded like a chuckle under his breath. Andrew and Ryder exchanged a look of confusion, but remained rooted to their spots.

Andrew groaned.

"Come on." Ryder grabbed his hand and pulled, but Andrew pulled it away. He didn't stop following him, though. "Yeah, Uncle Kyle?"

Uncle Kyle was tossing hay into the stall and didn't break stride. "Anything you boys want to tell me about what was going on back there?"

"Nothing in particular," Ryder responded coolly, but his words and tone belied his nervousness.

Mr. Kensington looked at them and leaned up against the wall, trying to look serious. He tried to meet Andrew's gaze, but Andrew refused to look him in the eye. He fixed his stare on a spot on the floor as if it were the most interesting thing in the barn. His heart raced. *So dead. So, so dead.*

"Boys, I expect you to know better," Uncle Kyle finally said after a few moments of excruciating silence.

"Uncle Kyle, we—"

"Hold on, I'm not finished. I expect you to know better than to mess around when you're working for me. The horses need to be cared for, and you're on my time." He let his voice go into an affected Southern drawl that sounded fake. Andrew looked at him and grew even more confused when his lips curled up into a smile. "Don't look so worried. It's okay. I already knew about the two of you. I figured it out a while ago, to be honest."

"You knew?" Ryder asked.

"Yes, I knew. And I'm okay with the two of you seeing each other. But I meant what I said about you working. The horses really do need to be looked after. However, when you're on your own…"

He didn't need to finish his sentence and went back to his work with the stall.

"You're right. We're sorry," Ryder said.

"Good. Now get back over there and get to work. I expect those stalls to be mucked out and finished within the hour."

"Yes, sir! And, Uncle Kyle? Thank you." Clearly relieved, Ryder dragged the still-gawking Andrew back to the stall. "Come on, Andy. Move it."

"What the…what the hell was that about?" Andy whispered.

"I told you it wouldn't be a problem," Ryder rasped back.

"He's going to tell your aunt, isn't he?"

Ryder picked up the shovel. "Probably. But if he's cool with it, then she will be, too."

"I really, really hope you're right."

Andrew followed Ryder's lead and finished the stall, but his actions felt clumsy as his mind raced. They were being stupid. They had to be more careful. Mr. Kensington had already figured it out before he caught them. Even if Mr. Kensington didn't mind, that didn't mean everyone else would be as forgiving.

CHAPTER EIGHTEEN

I can't believe my dad agreed to this!" Andrew said just two days later. He pushed Ryder's bag off the seat and onto the floor.

"I know. My aunt and uncle, too. It's great!"

It was nearly midnight on Christmas Eve and Andrew stopped at the Kensingtons' to pick up Ryder. His parents had spoken with the Kensingtons about the situation, and though they hesitated initially, they finally agreed to let Ryder stay with Andrew's family for the holiday. And now he was going to their house to spend the next three days with them. Just like they'd planned. Andrew had gotten back from Buffalo just twenty minutes earlier and had barely had time to put his gifts in the house before dashing out to collect Ryder and his things.

The slick snow that had been falling all day covered the road, and it definitely felt like Christmas. Ryder looked around as Andrew drove back to his house. Christmas songs were all over the radio, and Andrew sang along with them, unable to contain his excitement and holiday spirit.

"So how was your family today?"

"Crazy, but we had a lot of fun. A lot of good food, too. I'm so full."

"What kind of stuff did you get?"

Andrew laughed. "Clothes, a CD, DVD, some gift cards. Normal stuff from family members that don't know what to buy, you know? What about you? Did your aunt and uncle get you anything?"

"Yeah, we opened our stuff tonight. They got me some gift cards too, but the coolest thing? I got a package from my mom and dad."

"Really? That's great!"

"Yeah, Aunt Lisa got it a week ago, but she hid it from me so I'd wait to open it." He grinned. "She knew I would have opened it that day. They sent a letter and a bunch of pictures and souvenirs and things like that. Some books and a cool shirt."

"Books? Can you read German?"

"No, not at all. But it's still cool. Mom figured I'd like it. I think they'll make me look smarter."

"Dork," Andrew teased.

No one else traveled the roads this late at night with the snow on the ground. Andrew drove slowly with the truck in four-wheel drive, and close to forty-five minutes later pulled up to his house. The lights were already off in the living room, but the Christmas tree lights sparkled in the front window. The large tree completely took it over.

Quietly, the two brought Ryder's things into the house and locked the door behind them. "Where am I going to sleep?" asked Ryder.

"In the family room. Mom said we can both sleep in there if we want."

"Think that's a good idea?" Ryder teased as Andrew's face flushed visibly even in the dim light.

"Probably not. I should sleep upstairs tonight. But come on, I'll help you get the couch ready. It's not that bad."

"I don't mind. I'd sleep on the floor if I had to."

"Maybe in the summer, but it's too cold for that now."

Between the two of them they managed to get the couch made with the sheets and blankets his mother had left. Ryder tossed his pillow down and stretched.

"What time do you get up in the morning?"

"Pretty early. Everyone fights for the shower. Andrea's usually the last, though."

"Wake me when you get up?"

Andrew nodded. "Sure. I'm usually up by eight, is that all right?"

"That's fine."

Looking around the room, Andrew hesitated briefly before closing the distance between them and giving him a deep kiss. Ryder's hands settled briefly on his hips before they pulled away from each other.

"Night," Andrew whispered.

"Good night."

Andrew headed upstairs to get ready for bed. After changing in the bathroom, he slipped silently across the hall and collapsed onto his bed. The sheets were cold but warmed up quickly. Across the room Andrea had already fallen deeply asleep. With a sigh he turned toward the wall. *I want my room back,* he thought before he closed his eyes and fell asleep.

❖

Andrew woke up to smell of coffee drifting into his room. Without hesitating he threw back the covers and slid out of bed. His parents were already up, moving downstairs, and Andrea still slept soundly, as predicted. Grabbing his clothes, he made his way to the bathroom and took a quick shower. He wondered if Ryder had woken up yet as he dressed and brushed his hair. He dried it quickly and went downstairs to see. Ryder sat at the kitchen table with his father, holding a cup of coffee and wearing just his sweats.

"Morning," Andrew said calmly as he poured himself a cup of coffee. His heart pounded at having his boyfriend sitting at the table so early in the morning with his father.

Ryder grinned, already sipping from his. "Mornin'."

"You're up early."

"The delicious scent of coffee and bacon woke me," Ryder admitted. "Kind of hard to ignore your stomach."

"And you'll have your fill of it once you go shower," Andrew's mother said from the stove.

Ryder nodded and stood, setting his mug down. "I'll do that before Andrea gets up."

Andrew watched as he disappeared into the living room, then reappeared with a bundle of clothes and went upstairs. A few minutes later he heard the shower running.

"I hope that couch is comfortable enough," his father said.

"It is, don't worry," said Andrew. He stole a piece of bacon and slid away from the stove when his mother reached out to smack his arm.

"Stop stealing the food and go wake your sister."

Andrew dashed up the stairs and threw the door open. "Andrea! Mom says to wake up. It's Christmas."

No movement came from the other bed.

"Andrea!"

"Nghh, what?" came a muffled groan from the bed.

"Get your ass up. Mom's making breakfast, and Grandma and Grandpa are going to be here in like an hour. Get moving. Or me and Ryder are going to eat all of the bacon."

"It's so early," she whined, rolling onto her back and rubbing her eyes. She pushed herself up and yawned, hair sticking everywhere.

Behind him the shower stopped. "Shower's free. Ryder just got out."

Andrea glared at him but got out of bed and grabbed her clothes. Ryder opened the door and steam poured out into the hallway. He stood dressed in a new pair of jeans and a new shirt. His hair hung in wet, gently waved strands nearly to his shoulders.

Andrew followed him down the stairs.

"Is that the shirt your mom bought you?"

"Yep, pretty cool, isn't it?"

"Yeah, it's nice," Andrew admitted. He admired the way it clung to Ryder's taller frame in all the right places, showing off his thin but strong body and muscular arms.

With the showering out of the way they were allowed to eat their breakfast. The bacon was crisp and the pancakes were shaped vaguely like little trees. By the time Andrea came downstairs, dressed, everyone else had finished eating. A plate had been left out for her and she ate while everyone else cleaned up. Andrew's mom put the ham in the oven to start cooking and set it for a few hours.

"There, that will be ready by one," she said as she stepped back. She pushed them all out of the kitchen to get out of her way as she started to set up for later. They went to the living room and dropped onto the couch, staring at the tree with all its presents.

Andrew put in an old Christmas movie, *Scrooge*, and they watched it for a while. He knew all of the words and could sing all of the songs, and explained to Ryder that he would only watch that version of *Scrooge* on Christmas day. When his grandparents arrived, Andrew's grandfather came in and started singing with the movie as well, striking goofy poses as he did so. Ryder laughed along with everyone else.

After their arrival the family stopped to open presents. Though only six of them were present, there were a lot of gifts under the tree, most having been shipped in from out-of-state family and friends. Ryder sat next to Andrew, content to watch.

Andrew watched Ryder from the corner of his eye. He could tell that although he had a smile on his face, it was strained. He missed his own parents, and Andrew wished they were here with him; he couldn't begin to imagine what it would be like not to have your parents around for the holiday.

"Thanks, Grandma! These are great," he said as he shed his old shoes to pull the brand-new pair on.

"You're welcome. Glad you like them."

"Here you go, Ryder," Andrew's mother said as she handed him a small box.

He took it, confusion sweeping across his face. "What's this?"

"Open it and find out."

Ryder glanced over at Andrew who shrugged, fighting back a grin. "Mr. and Mrs. Morris, you didn't have to get me anything."

"We wanted to. Just open it."

He did as they asked and grinned at the gift card inside the box. It was for the local sports store that carried riding tack. "Hey, thanks! This is great."

"We saw that they carried horse supplies, but we weren't sure what you needed."

"This is fantastic. Cobalt needs a new halter. Thank you!"

They continued opening gifts. During the small lulls where they were admiring what had been given to them, Andrew's grandparents talked to Ryder about his horse. He told them about how he had brought Cobalt up from Texas and how long the trip had been.

"The ham should be ready, so let's eat now," said Andrew's mother as she stood up. "We'll open the stockings after."

Everyone filed into the dining room and took their seats. Andrew motioned for Ryder to sit next to him before excusing himself. He headed upstairs with the pretense of using the bathroom, but stopped quickly into his room first and retrieved Ryder's gift. After sneaking downstairs he hid the gift in the branches of the Christmas tree and then rejoined his family at the table.

Everyone took their time eating the delicious food, but it wasn't long after that they moved on to the living room and conversation from dinner carried over.

"Have you kids decided where you're going for college?" Andrew's grandmother asked, sipping a cup of tea. "You should have sent your applications in by now, right?"

"We've decided," Andrea said proudly, and Andrew glanced at her in alarm.

"You did?" his father and mother asked simultaneously.

"Yes," Andrea replied, not looking at Andrew. "We're both accepting the scholarships to UConn."

"Congrat—" his grandfather started, but Andrew cut him off.

"Wait a second! I didn't say that. I said I wanted to go to Utica College. I already filled out the paperwork. I just haven't gotten the official acceptance letter yet."

"What made you decide on Utica?" his grandfather asked.

"I didn't want soccer to be my main focus."

"UConn is a better school!" Andrea shouted, standing up. "I already sent out our applications!"

"You what?" Andrew demanded, standing as well. "You

actually filled it out for me? That's forgery, Andrea! You could get in trouble for that!"

"Well, *you* certainly weren't filling it out. What was I supposed to do?"

"I told you, I don't want—"

"That's enough," their father commanded, and they both froze at the tone in his voice. "It's Christmas. We're not getting into this today. We'll discuss it later."

Nervously, their grandmother shifted her attention to Ryder. "What are you going to do about college, Ryder?"

Ryder looked up from his hands, briefly glancing at Andrew before answering. "I…don't know yet. I haven't really thought about it. I might take a year off. Maybe go visit my parents in Germany."

"What about going to school over there?"

"I don't speak German."

"Well, there are American colleges over there, too."

"Maybe…" Ryder said and looked at Andrew again.

Andrew focused intently on the floor, pretending to listen to the conversation, though his mind raced between thoughts of his sister's subterfuge and possibilities with Ryder. Unfortunately, not many of his thoughts ended the way he wanted—with Ryder attending college in Utica with him.

"But I still have time to decide. I don't even know what I'd want to major in yet."

❖

While the family moved on to opening the stockings that hung over the fireplace, Andrew found himself stuck on thoughts of Andrea and college. His father might have wanted to discuss it later, but that didn't put it out of his mind. What was Andrea's deal? Sure she'd always been a little bossy, but to actually fill out his application and send it in? This went far beyond anything she had ever done before.

"Andrew, are you all right?" his mother asked as he held the tube of hot chocolate–flavored Chapstick in his hand absently.

"Yes, sorry," Andrew replied, embarrassed by having been caught. He opened the tube and rolled it onto his lips, forcing a grin. "Mmm, tastes just like I had a cup," he said and everyone laughed.

Ryder grinned and Andrew could almost hear his thoughts echoing in his mind. He fought to control a blush and, for the moment, thoughts of college were put out of his mind. The twins each got an iTunes gift card, and when they both thanked their parents, they shot each other a glare and fell silent. Andrew's mother handed Ryder a small envelope. He looked quizzically at it but opened it and thanked her; he had gotten one as well.

"Andrew said you did have an iPod."

He nodded. "I do, thank you."

When they were finished and everyone had started into their candy, Andrew wondered when he would get a chance to sneak away from the tense atmosphere surrounding Andrea and give Ryder his gift. He got his chance when his grandfather and mother got up to get dessert. Andrew announced that he'd be right back and tugged discreetly on Ryder's sleeve as he passed behind him. Ryder followed Andrew into the family room where his things were stored in the corner.

After reaching into the branches of the tree and retrieving the gift, Andrew stood awkwardly in the middle of the room by the couch and shifted from foot to foot while Ryder rooted around in his bag. When he stood, Andrew held out the small box to him.

"Here…I…it's not much. But I thought you might like it, and, well. Here," he said, tripping over his words. Ryder grinned and took it, then handed the larger box to him.

"Same. I saw it and thought of you, so I hope you like it."

Andrew's face flushed and he nodded as he took the present. They both sat down on the couch, ripping into the wrapping.

Ryder pulled out a small box and took off the cover, then grinned. "It's Cobalt. At least, it looks like him."

"Do you like it?" asked Andrew, anxious.

"Yeah, I do. Thanks. And I needed a watch, too." He pulled the watch out of the box and put it on. Painted inside the watch face, a ghostly image of a horse that looked like Cobalt stood proudly.

"It's waterproof."

"Great, now I can ride in all weather and not worry about it," he said with amusement.

Missing the teasing tone, relief coursed through Andrew that the gift seemed to be appropriate, and he finally opened his box.

Inside rested a silver picture frame with his name engraved on it. The picture in the frame was one of him riding on Magpie, his face bright with laughter. He wasn't looking at the camera for the shot because he hadn't known it had been taken. He looked questioningly up at Ryder.

"My uncle took it. I asked him to."

"It's a great shot," Andrew said, voice lowered in awe. He ran his hand over the picture and smiled. "I had no idea. Thanks, I love it. It's great." He did love it, but he wondered where he'd be able to put it. Andrea would know who it was from, and she would question it. When had he gotten it? When had it been taken? He leaned closer to the picture and examined it. Even he could see how happy he looked to be there. But it wasn't just happiness from feeling free and racing around on the back of a horse.

"You really like it?" Ryder asked, pulling him from his thoughts.

Andrew nodded and looked up at him with a smile on his face. "Yeah, I do. I swear." Ryder looked as relieved as Andrew had felt, and he set down the picture. He leaned over on the couch and Ryder leaned toward him. They met in a brief kiss before pulling away.

"I was worried. You looked lost for a moment there."

"What?"

Ryder poked the side of his face gently. "You looked so serious. If you like the picture, then what is it?"

Andrew sighed. As if he could keep anything from Ryder. "I'm just worried what Andrea will think when she sees it. She's so...off lately."

"Who cares what she thinks. It's not about her. Come on, let's go back. I think someone mentioned dessert."

Ryder stood and strolled into the other room where Andrew's family was chatting happily. Andrew heard the clink of forks on plates and happy laughter. He set the picture down on the table—Ryder was right, who cared what she thought—but he still felt uneasy as he followed his boyfriend into the other room.

CHAPTER NINETEEN

After dessert, everyone picked up the trash and stowed their gifts. The men got out their boots and other winter gear, pulled it on, and made a trek up to the barn in the back. On the way, Andrew glanced up at the tree house and frowned. The heavy snow had accumulated on it, and the roof hung even lower than it had just a week ago. If they got another big storm, it would be gone. But Andrew could not do anything about it now.

His father pulled back the barn doors and they followed him inside. Just to the right were a pile of sleds and the other winter weather toys. Two inflatable tubes lay jumbled inside a box, and he pulled them out, checking them over for any rips, holes, or tears. "Not sure if they are still good or not. I should have kept them in the attic. Oh well, let's see if we can get these blown up."

After they carried their finds back down, his father pulled out the portable compressor from his car and set it up. They got it working and inflated the two tubes. Much to his surprise, both tubes filled with air and held it in. Andrew's mother and grandmother had stayed at the house to make a large batch of hot chocolate for later. In an hour or so they would drive down with the steaming cocoa to meet them at the hill; until then, everyone else would walk down with their own sleds.

Despite having complained about her stomach not ten minutes before when she'd decided to stay in the house, Andrea seemed well enough to join them. She didn't talk directly to Andrew, though, as she walked with her grandfather. She kept the discussion firmly on UConn and the excellent scholarship opportunity.

"You see," she said loudly enough for everyone in their party to hear, "it's not just about sports, really. UConn is a top school academically. Anyone offered a scholarship with them should consider themselves lucky."

Andrew sped up and tried to tune her out.

Holding the inflatable tubes as they walked, Ryder suddenly turned and started to smack Andrew with his. Stunned, Andrew stood there for a moment, taking a second blow before he reacted and lashed out at Ryder. They laughed and ran ahead of the group chasing after each other.

When a snowball hit Ryder in the middle of the back he dropped the tube and started to make his own, winding up to aim it straight for Andrea's smirking face. She shrieked and ducked behind her father, but Ryder couldn't stop himself in time.

It hit him dead center in the chest.

Laughing, they all dropped what they were holding and had an impromptu snowball fight in the middle of the road. The snow fell lightly, adding to the foot and a half already on the ground as they tossed the wet snow back and forth. Andrea grabbed her saucer and used it as a shield. Her grandfather and father ducked behind it as she held it up.

It felt good to fool around, Andrew decided, despite the earlier blowout he and Andrea had. Maybe later they would be able to sit down and talk about it rationally. He hoped.

"Hey! That's cheating," Ryder yelled, breaking into his reverie. He held an armload of snowballs and let a barrage of them go. The sound of wet snow hitting plastic echoed in the nearly silent air. Andrew laughed hard and struggled to catch his breath. He finally dropped down onto the snowbank at the side of the road, gasping for air.

Ryder flopped onto his back next to him for a moment, grinning. One last round of snowballs pelted him, and then they stopped as well.

"That's the most fun I've had in ages! Too bad the girls missed that," his grandfather said with a sparkle in his eyes, speaking about his daughter and wife.

Andrew's father laughed and helped haul the boys to their feet. Andrew leaned against Ryder for a few moments, still breathless from laughing so hard. "You should have seen your face when they used the saucer as a shield," he said, and broke into a fit of giggles. He coughed and finally caught his breath, wiping his streaming eyes.

"Glad I could be everyone's entertainment. Thank you, I'll be here all week," he said with a low bow. They chuckled and started for the hill again.

The hill stood at the end of the road with cars parked off to one side on the nearly level ground. Kids screamed and shrieked with delight as they slid down the hill on new sleds and tried to avoid crashing into others, or stood at the bottom trying to dodge the kids that were coming down. At the steepest part of the hill a group of kids made a chain and pushed off down the hill. Halfway down it broke off into smaller sections when the force became too much for them to continue holding on. They all ended up heading toward the slushy marsh.

Ryder and Andrew watched with the adults as the lead kids in each chain forged a path through the reeds and bushes, unable to stop the momentum they carried. The rest of the chain followed them into the tunnels they made, and those up on the hill could see the carnage as the leaders slowed to a stop and the rest of the kids plowed into them.

A few of the parents stumbled down the hill to help them out, but most stood at the top, laughing. It took a few minutes, but eventually all of the kids were pulled out. When they started back up the hill, Ryder saw that some of them were covered in mud.

"What's that? I thought it would be snowy."

"Oh, they must have broken through the ice in the marsh. It's like a bog in there. That's why there are so many reeds and cattails," Andrew explained. "Nasty stuff to get caught in. Come on, let's go down."

The two of them set up the tubes at a high spot on the hill.

Andrea joined them, and her father stood behind her. When they pushed off, their father reached out and spun Andrea, laughing as she shrieked and tried to keep herself from spinning. Andrew ended up facing up the hill as he slid backward, despite trying to lean into a turn.

Once they reached the base of the hill, the three of them trudged back up to the top as the two adults in their group took their turns and flew past them down the hill. Andrew and Ryder turned to watch. Ryder turned back just in time to hear a kid scream "Look out!" and dove out of the way. He landed on his face in the snow and Andrea ran to help him.

"Are you all right?"

"Yeah, I'm fine," he said, spitting out a mouthful of snow.

"Never turn your back on the top of the hill. Half the kids here don't know how to steer, and even if they can, it's still hard sometimes." She laughed.

Ryder smiled. "Duly noted."

While Andrea was preoccupied with Ryder, Andrew picked up a snowball and lobbed it at her. She screamed as it hit her and chased him back up the hill, both of them laughing the whole way up. They collapsed from the exertion after they reached their space and all Andrea could manage was a halfhearted attempt at a throw. It missed Andrew by a foot.

Half an hour later Andrew's mother and grandmother arrived with a large thermos of hot chocolate. They poured small cups for everyone and chatted with neighbors as they leaned against the truck and drank the cocoa. His grandmother watched her husband go down the hill twice and shook her head in amusement.

"He thinks he's still young," she said fondly.

His mother smiled and shrugged. "Let Dad have his fun. It's good for him."

They stayed a little longer before heading back. The two women drove the truck with the men sitting in the back with the sleds and tubes. The twins and Ryder elected to walk back.

Though it was still afternoon, dark clouds filled the sky and more snow floated through the air. They walked well away from the road this time, trudging through the thick snow that covered the ground.

"I'm so taking a shower when we get home," declared Andrea as she tripped yet again. She shivered and wrapped her arms around herself. For the time being, her thoughts of college seemed to be suspended, which thrilled Andrew.

"I just want to get out of these wet clothes," he said, squeezing his hands together. His gloves were warm from his body heat, but still wet from the melted snow. "I hope Dad got a good fire going in the family room."

"I'll have a nice warm place to sleep," Ryder mused.

Just over a small rise the house came into view. From the chimney a thick plume of smoke billowed, and they hurried toward it. In the driveway the truck sat, still warm, as it settled with an assortment of clinks and clicks. When they pushed open the door they were greeted by a blast of warm air and the smell of fresh apple pie.

"Leave all your wet stuff by the door!" their mother called from the other room. They noticed the pile already there and quickly added to it. Andrea bolted for the stairs and the bathroom door slammed shut behind her.

"I'd say she is really looking forward to a hot shower, wouldn't you?" Ryder drawled, amused. Andrew nodded and followed upstairs at a calmer pace. Once in his room he shut the door behind them and started digging through his dresser for dry clothes.

Ryder slipped up behind him and wrapped his arms around his waist. Andrew straightened and felt light kisses drop on the back of his neck. He shivered and turned in his arms to return the kiss. Ryder backed him up to the bed and they fell onto it, a tangle of arms and legs. After a moment, Andrew shoved him off, panting for breath.

"Ryder, we can't. Not here," he hissed. He sprang off his bed and occupied himself with a clothes search again.

"Andrea's in the shower," Ryder pointed out with a gesture toward the door.

"And my parents or grandparents could come upstairs at any second."

"Your stairs creak and the pipes are loud enough that we'd hear the water stopping."

"You can't hear anything if you get too excited. You didn't hear your uncle approach us the last time."

Ryder had the grace to look embarrassed for a moment.

Andrew threw a shirt at him and changed out of his clothes, completely comfortable with Ryder watching. He left the soaked pile on the floor and then turned to Ryder, hands on his hips.

"If you're wet, get off my bed. I don't need to sleep in a puddle tonight."

Ryder sat up, making a show of wringing his shirt onto the bed after he pulled it off. Andrew grabbed it and tossed it on the pile, then handed him a T-shirt. The shirt fit tightly across his broad chest, but it looked great and showed off his arms even better than the last one he wore. Andrew had to remind himself not to stare as he followed him down the stairs into the living room.

His mother called him into the kitchen and cut him a slice of still-warm pie. He grabbed a second one for Ryder and waited in the other room. When Ryder came out of the bathroom, he had dressed in a dry pair of jeans and settled on the floor next to him. They turned on the television and watched *Rudolph* while they ate the pie. The day reminded him so much of being a kid, and he wished momentarily that things were just as easy as they had been when he was ten. *So much to worry about now. College. Andrea. Dating Ryder. Getting found out. If only it were easy again.*

Charlie called later that evening and asked about what they'd gotten. Andrew talked with him for a bit while Ryder dozed on the couch in a light sleep.

Andrew's grandparents left a few hours after that to head back home and wished them all a Merry Christmas again. They hugged everyone, including Ryder, as they left.

"Drive carefully," his mother said and waved from the front door. A blast of cold wind blew into the house and stirred the flames in the fireplace. "I hope the storm holds off a bit longer."

"The weatherman said it's going to blow over, but to expect a big one for New Year's," his father said from his armchair.

"Maybe we'll have to change our plans, then."

"Don't worry about it. The party is just down the road," his father replied.

Andrea got a call from a few of her friends and went out to visit one of them to exchange gifts. As she left she called out that she'd be back later. Andrew's parents sat down with the boys to watch another Christmas movie before heading up to bed themselves.

Once they were alone, Ryder held out an arm and Andrew slid closer, allowing himself the comfort of resting his head against Ryder's shoulder. Ryder's fingers slipped into his hair. It felt nice and comfortable and everything right. He closed his eyes, tired from the day, and swore he'd rest just a minute. When he opened his eyes again, the fire had died down and Ryder's fingers were no longer in his hair. He glanced up at him and saw that he had also fallen asleep. A little alarmed that they could have been caught, he pulled himself out of Ryder's arms and stood. Ryder shifted and lay down on the couch, still mostly asleep. Andrew grabbed a blanket and tossed it over him, then headed upstairs to his own room.

Andrea, luckily, had not yet returned, so he crawled into bed. Once he had settled onto his back, he stared up at the ceiling. Spending Christmas with Ryder had been great. If it hadn't been for Andrea causing trouble, it would have been perfect. A nagging feeling grew in his stomach, but he couldn't pinpoint what it was about. *Probably college and having to deal with Andrea.* Their conversation wasn't finished, and he didn't look forward to the rest of it. But it would be okay. It would blow over. He worried too much; things were just fine.

CHAPTER TWENTY

A ndrew was glad Ryder had a great time with his family, and when his aunt and uncle came back, he didn't want to leave. The horses had been cared for in their absence by one of the hired hands, but Cobalt would be missing him. Ryder made Andrew promise that he would come over soon to go riding, which of course he agreed to.

With Ryder gone, the house became much quieter. Even Andrea had gotten used to having him there and his mother missed the extra hand around. After he left, Andrew found himself cornered as she rambled on about how polite and well-spoken Ryder was, and how much he reminded her of his mother. Unknown to her, though, he had also acted as a buffer between the twins because Andrea kept her complaints to a minimum, much to Andrew's relief.

Charlie came over the next day with plans for New Year's Eve. A party had been set up down at the old campgrounds in the next town over. Fireworks had been purchased—and though it went unsaid in front of the parents, alcohol—and just about everyone from their school was going to be there. Sarah had already said she would go, and Charlie's next stop was Ryder's place.

"Sure, we'll be there," said Andrew.

"Cool, I'll let everyone know. Bring anything if you can, but we should have plenty."

He waved as he left, jogging out to his car, and backed out of the driveway with tires spinning on the slick pavement.

"Was that Charlie?" his mother asked as she poked her head around the corner of the kitchen. He nodded. "He left already?"

"Yeah, he just came to ask about New Year's Eve. There's going to be a party in the old campground in Stonington. I told him we'd go, is that all right?"

"That's fine…as long as you're careful. And no drinking," she warned, looking at him sternly.

Andrew held up a hand innocently. "I promise, Mom. We won't drink. I'm sure there won't be anything there, anyway."

She hesitated but nodded and disappeared back into the kitchen.

❖

The next few days of Christmas vacation went quicker than Andrew would have liked. After finding a printout of majors for UConn students on the foot of his bed one morning he began to sleep in each day and only got up once he knew Andrea had left with her friends. He had become adept at avoiding Andrea as much as possible until he knew how to handle the college situation. Once he went riding with Ryder when the weather had warmed, and the other days Ryder came over to his place and they hung out and watched movies all day. Through it all, no one suspected anything. Andrew's mother began to think of him as a fixture in her house, and his father appreciated the help he offered with the more labor-intensive chores of splitting and carrying wood. Andrew felt more comfortable in their relationship, and snuck kisses whenever they were alone— even if one of his family members was just in the next room.

When New Year's Eve finally arrived, Andrew and Andrea got ready for the night and bundled up in their warmest clothing. Their parents were still home to see them off and were getting ready themselves for the party at their neighbor's house just down the road.

"Remember, no drinking," warned their mother for the fiftieth time that day.

"We won't," they answered in unison, rolling their eyes.

"And if you need us, call. We'll have our cell phones, but you can also call the Jacksons' house. You know their phone number."

"Mom, we get it."

"We'll be home shortly after midnight, okay? Don't stay out too late. And come home if you're not feeling comfortable, or if anything happens."

"Alice, really. That's enough," his father said, steering his wife away from them. "Have fun, kids. Just be responsible."

"Thanks, Dad."

Andrew grabbed his keys off the table and Andrea shut the door behind them. Snow fell lightly but the weatherman predicted that it would only get worse. There wouldn't be any fireworks if it didn't stop. Once in the truck, they headed out to pick up Ryder before the drive out to Stonington.

"Have you come to your senses yet?" Andrea asked as she sat across the cab, her arms folded against her chest to keep warm.

"My senses about what?" Andrew asked, though he knew where the conversation was going. He sighed. It had taken her long enough to corner him on it. He'd already held off the discussion for as long as he could.

"About UConn. We'll get our acceptance letters next month."

"I didn't even write the essay. How could you do that?"

"Because you were being stupid about it!" she yelled, throwing her hands into the air. She turned to look at Andrew, her eyes narrowed. She reached forward and gripped the dashboard directly in front of her. "You don't get it, do you? UConn is such a good school and you're going to throw away a great opportunity for what? To go to Utica? Grow up, Andrew. You need to get out of this small town and live a little!" Her breath came out in giant puffs of steam and threatened to fog the windows with all her excitement. Andrew tried to keep his focus on the road.

"No, you grow up. We can't always be together. I don't want to go out of state. What's the big deal? It's not like we'll be in the same classes in college."

"We could be, at least for our undergrad courses. We can sign up for classes at the same time. It will make the transition easier for you."

"Andrea, this is ridiculous."

He didn't have to continue the conversation because at that moment they pulled up to Ryder's house and saw him waiting for them on the porch, jumping up and down. He rushed at the truck before Andrew had put it in park and threw open the door.

"Shit, it's cold out!" he complained.

"Why weren't you waiting inside?" Andrew asked as he cranked up the heat. Andrea reluctantly slid over and let Ryder in, though she kept closer to him than Andrew.

"I knew you'd be here any minute. Is something going on?" he asked as he shut the door.

"No," they both answered.

The drive to the campground took about half an hour from the Kensingtons' farm, and by the time they got there, dozens of other vehicles had parked in the plowed-out area.

Andrew found a spot near the road and shut down the ignition. Charlie saw them get out and waved them over, holding a red plastic cup.

"Hey! You're here," he said with a lopsided grin.

"Obviously." Andrea snorted. Sarah held on to Charlie's arm, laughing. She held a red cup as well and waved it at them.

"Drinks are in the pavilion. Hey, Ryder."

Ryder nodded. "Hey."

"They had to cancel the fireworks because it's too wet. But they're going to do them on the second if the storm clears by then."

"We'll have to come out again," Andrew said, and made his way toward the pavilion. Ryder trailed after him, and people they knew from school stopped them on the way to chat and catch up. They had to speak loudly over the heavy bass of the music coming from a smaller gazebo just past the pavilion. Andrew introduced Ryder to the people he knew from Stonington. Most of them were on the soccer teams, and a few others he knew from mutual friends' parties.

When they finally reached the pavilion, someone asked what they wanted to drink. Ryder grabbed a soda, insisting he didn't want a drink, but Andrew grabbed a cup of beer. He took a sip from it and made a face.

"Watered-down," he responded when Ryder looked questioningly at him.

"Don't drink it, then."

Andrew shrugged and sipped at it as they mingled with the crowd. Karina was there, and she winked at the two of them and motioned them over. Andrew groaned when Ryder followed her to the edge of the field, away from anyone they knew.

"So?" she asked when they were alone.

Ryder grinned and gave her the thumbs-up.

Karina squealed her excitement and gave them both hugs. "Congrats, guys! I promise I won't tell anyone. Your secret is safe with me."

Andrew looked around and saw a few people lingering at the edge of the field near them. He swallowed nervously, wondering if they heard her outburst. When they didn't glance over he assumed they hadn't, but he motioned for her to keep it down anyway.

"That's cool, but uh, what's with the squealing?" Ryder asked, slinging an arm around both of their shoulders. Some of his soda splashed onto the ground.

"I think it's cute. I love adorable gay guys." Before either of them could protest, she winked and slipped out from under Ryder's arm and bolted back to the party.

Adorable gay guys? Andrew stared after her, rolling the word over in his mind. Was that what he really was? Gay? He'd never thought about it like that. He just liked Ryder. He liked spending time with him and seeing him, and yeah, kissing him.

Gay.

The word sent a jolt through his chest, a tingling sensation that spread to his palms and down his legs. It made him jittery, almost nervous, but not quite. Andrew glanced at his palms before he watched her go, shaking his head. "Karina. Who knew?"

"She's cool. I like her."

"Yeah, she's awesome. But a little loud." He glanced around for a second time to make sure no one was watching. One girl had glanced their way and stared at them. Andrew's stomach dropped, but when her friends called her name she turned back to them and laughed at their joke.

She probably didn't hear anything.

They made their way back to the party and found Andrea. She chatted with Michael and Karina. Ryder looked around and asked if Melissa had come, but she hadn't. This sort of party wasn't her thing, though Karina had asked her to come out.

As the time neared midnight, Andrew had ditched his drink and got a new cup for soda. Sipping on the flat Pepsi, he joked around with everyone. Charlie was completely wasted and unsteady on his feet, and he had to lean heavily on Sarah. She laughed with him, but Ryder made a face at the whole display and started to wander off. Andrew got up and followed him, calling out to get him to stop.

"Hey! Wait for me," he said and dropped his cup in the trash barrel. Ryder had his hands shoved deep in his pockets, though he kept glancing at his watch. "Aren't you having fun?"

"It's all right," he said and glanced around. "But it's not much of a party."

"Yeah, sucks about the fireworks." He followed Ryder out behind the main building and glanced around. They were alone, though he could hear people talking nearby and the music still filled the cold air. Ryder leaned against the building and pulled Andrew close to him.

"Ryder...people are all over the place."

"There's no one here right now. Relax," he said and refused to let him go. Andrew realized he was losing an uphill battle and stopped fighting. Besides, he *wanted* to kiss Ryder. He leaned against him and tilted his head up for a kiss when he felt a hand under his chin.

Soft and sweet lips pressed gently against his, and Andrew let himself be drawn deeper into it. He closed his eyes and pressed closer, enjoying the feel of Ryder's warm hands sliding up under his jacket and shirt to press against his bare skin. Ryder shifted his legs and spread them into a wider stance, inviting Andrew to stand inside the space they made, and he did. He lost himself in the moment and forgot they were in a public place where anyone could see them, but for that minute, it didn't matter. All the sounds faded away to muted silence; the only things he heard were the rushing of his pulse and their soft breaths.

He didn't notice the footsteps coming from around the corner of the building until it was too late. When he heard the sharp gasp, he jerked his head back and waited for the worst. And it really couldn't have gotten any worse.

Right at the corner of the building stood his sister, with her eyes wide and one hand frozen on the side of the wooden structure. She stared at them with a mixture of shocked fascination and horror. Andrew felt his own face color despite the cold, and then pale. He felt sick and dizzy. Ryder swore softly under his breath.

"Andrea—"

"Oh, my God," she said, and turned to leave just as suddenly as she came. Andrew waited a second before rushing after her with Ryder close behind.

"Andrea, wait!"

"I want to go home!" she yelled as she dodged everyone in her path. She ran to the truck, opened the door, and climbed inside. Andrew climbed awkwardly into the driver's seat. Ryder started to climb into the passenger seat when Andrea pushed him back out. "No. You find your own ride home."

"Andrea! We brought him here. I'm not going to make him—"

"I don't want him touching me! He can walk home for all I care!" she screamed, and a few people closer to the cars turned to look in their direction.

"Andrea, you're making a scene," Andrew whispered.

"Look, I can catch a ride with Karina if it's a problem," Ryder started, holding his hands up.

"No, get in the truck. I'll bring you home."

"I said—"

"Andrea! Knock it off. I'm giving Ryder a ride home."

She remained locked in fuming silence.

Andrew blew out his frustration. "If you want, I'll take him home and then come back and get you," Andrew reasoned. A few of their friends had started toward them, concern on their faces. *No, not this. Please not this. Not now.*

"I am not staying here. Take me home right now, Andrew."

"Andrea, look—"

"I don't want to hear it," she said, cutting him off again.

Andrew swallowed hard and started the truck. He motioned for Ryder to hurry up and get in as a small crowd started to gather behind the truck. Andrea seemed to realize everyone had focused their attention on them and stopped her protesting when Ryder climbed in. She centered herself on the seat and crossed her arms tightly over her chest, avoiding touching either of them. Andrew drove back into town and turned down the road for the Kensingtons' farm. All the lights were off in the house when they pulled up. Ryder got out of the truck and hesitated before shutting the door.

"I'll call you?"

Andrew nodded and gave him a small, tight smile. Ryder looked worried as they drove off.

With Ryder out of the car, Andrea moved over as far as she could. She leaned against the door, not looking at her brother. Andrew's heart pounded in his chest, and he felt sick. He'd made a stupid mistake and now he would pay for it.

The snow fell heavily by the time they reached their house, and the roads were getting slicker by the second. It was hard enough driving with the road conditions, but his shaking hands made it worse.

When he pulled into the driveway, all the lights were on downstairs. *Great, Mom and Dad are home*, he thought. *This is not going to be good.*

Andrea didn't bother shutting the door as she leapt from the truck and bolted for the house. The door slammed behind her as she entered, and Andrew stayed in his seat for a few minutes, steeling himself for a confrontation. Large flakes of snow drifted into the cab and landed on the seat and dashboard, melting from the heat.

When the front door opened and his father looked out, he reluctantly got out of the truck, shut the doors, and slowly made his way up the house while trying to keep a calm look on his face. He stopped in front of his father.

"What the hell is wrong with your sister? Did something happen out there? She just came in spouting all this stuff and yelling. We can barely understand her. Did someone try something with her?"

"No, Dad. Nothing happened to her. She's fine."

His father opened the door wider and let him in, and Andrew stepped inside. He set his keys down on the table and started to unzip his jacket when Andrea and his mother came around the corner from the living room.

"Mom, Dad, your *son* has something he wants to tell you."

They all looked at him and he tensed. "No I don't. I don't know what she's talking about," he said, but his cheeks started to burn and he couldn't stop them. He thought for sure he was about to be sick all over the floor. His stomach clenched tightly and the shaking in his hands moved down to his knees. He leaned against the door frame to stay on his feet.

"Yes, you do!" she screamed, stomping up to him, just inches away from his face "I saw you! Don't deny it. I know what I saw. I wasn't drinking!"

"Andrew, what is she talking about?"

"Nothing, she's not talking about anything. Andrea, let's talk about this, please? Alone?" he pleaded, reaching out to grab her hand. They'd always confided in each other, so why would she tell them like this without talking to him about it first? Why couldn't they discuss this like the rational people they always had been?

Because Andrea hadn't been rational lately. Ever since the stupid scholarships came along.

"Nothing? No, we're not talking about this alone. It's so disgusting, I can't even…Mom, Dad," she said, turning toward them, "I saw Ryder and Andrew kissing. And I don't mean like…

like friends kissing on the cheek. I mean like they were *kissing* and really getting into it."

Andrew narrowed his eyes, barely able to control the anger that rose within him, and he suppressed his desire to be sick.

His parents turned as one to stare at him. His mother's eyes were wide and begged him to deny it. A sharp gasp escaped past her open lips. Her face turned pale, almost ghostly, and then colored to the brightest shade of red. His father's expression was guarded and unreadable, though there was a small flicker of surprise in his eyes. His lips pressed into a firm line.

"Andrew, is that true?" his mother asked in a nearly inaudible whisper.

He sighed and took a deep breath before letting it out. What could he do? What *should* he do? Andrea would convince his parents, and he wouldn't be able to keep denying it, would he? Maybe for now, but when would it slip out again? He couldn't keep it from them, or himself, anymore. This wasn't fair. He should be able to tell them when he was ready, not because Andrea was forcing his hand. "Yeah, it's true."

"Oh, my God," his mother cried, hand flying up to her mouth. "Andrew…"

He cringed and looked up at his father, expecting the worst.

"I can't believe it," Andrea yelled. "You're gay! All this time dating all those girls and sleeping with them, and you're a fag? What a joke! You've lied to me this whole time!"

"Andrea, that's enough," Dad warned. "I will not tolerate that kind of language in this house."

"No, that's not enough, Dad. Are you sleeping with Ryder, too? Is it just like being with Cynthia?"

His mother burst into tears and left the room, her hands covering her face.

Andrew looked down at the ground, unable to speak. Anger and shock from her violent response to all of this coursed through his body. But his hesitation seemed to give her more fuel for the fire, and she continued. "Oh God," she whispered. "He's turned *you—*"

"Andrea! That is enough!" his father yelled. "Get upstairs and cool off!"

Andrew couldn't stick around to find out what would happen next, so he grabbed his keys, threw the door open, and ran out of the house.

His father ran onto the driveway and called for him, but Andrew had already backed the truck out of the driveway and set the tires spinning. When his father's hand hit the tailgate of the truck, Andrew ignored him and continued his race down the road, needing to get away as quickly as possible.

CHAPTER TWENTY-ONE

Andrew stood on the Kensingtons' porch, banging on the door, still trying to calm his racing pulse. A full minute later, the porch lights flickered on and Ryder opened the door. Based on what he wore, Andrew knew that Ryder had already gone to bed. He knew he looked like crap too, as he shivered in the wind.

"Andrew, what the hell?" Ryder grabbed him, dragged him inside, and then shut the door behind them. Once inside, Ryder dragged him over to the fireplace and stood in front of it with him. Andrew shivered violently again and wrapped his arms around himself.

"What happened?"

"Andrea. She told my parents," he groaned. "After I dropped you off, she didn't talk to me the entire way home. And as soon as I parked the truck, she bolted for the house and just exploded! She asked if we were having sex in front of my parents, and I couldn't deny it. Oh God, Ryder. She told my parents. I can't believe she told them!"

Ryder jerked back liked Andrew's words physically assaulted him. "Shit! Andrew, I'm so sorry they found out this way. Are you okay?" he asked, wrapping his arms around Andrew and pulling him close. "How did they take it?"

"I didn't stick around to wait and see what they would say. I got the hell out of there."

Ryder pulled back to look at him. "In this storm? You could have been killed, Andy."

"I *couldn't* stay!" Andrew argued. "My mother started crying and Andrea freaked out. My dad...I don't even want to know what he's going to do when I get home." He pushed away, out of Ryder's warm arms, and started to pace around the room. "Why couldn't my parents be cool like your uncle?"

Ryder followed him as he paced, trying to catch up with him, but Andrew evaded him. He wanted his comfort but didn't think he'd be able to hold himself together if he got it. "Not all parents are. I'm sorry, Andy. I really am. I shouldn't have kissed you there."

"You thought we were alone. It's not your fault. I could have pushed you away, but I didn't." Andrew sighed and shook his head, defeated. "Look, can I stay here tonight?"

"Of course. Tomorrow we'll figure out what we're going to do."

"We?"

"You think I'm going to be a jerk and let you go through this alone?"

"But before..."

"You mean what happened in Texas? That was different. My parents aren't around, okay? We'll talk to Uncle Kyle in the morning and figure something out. Andrea saw me, too. It's going to get out anyway. Better to have the two of us together than face this alone, right?" Ryder offered him a weak smile.

Andrew sighed and looked up at him, his eyes red and slightly swollen from crying in the truck. Ryder pulled him into his arms and kissed his forehead. "Let's get you a cup of tea or something."

"I don't drink tea."

"It's warm and it'll calm you down. You're drinking it now," he said and smiled.

Andrew sat down on the couch while Ryder went into the kitchen. He could hear him fill the kettle with water and set it loudly on the glass stovetop. The sound of the cabinets opening and closing followed by a tin popping open filled his senses as he let his mind wander.

Did I leave too quickly? Dad didn't really seem that upset. Maybe he was just worried. Andrew shook his head. *No way, I'm just imagining that. He's pissed, just like Andrea. And Mom...Mom looked so miserable. She heard every word Andrea said. Oh God, did she really have to bring that up? I've never mentioned anything like that to them. I've always kept it secret. Why did she have to tell them that?* Andrew cringed as his thoughts flew. What were his parents thinking about right now? Were they thinking about their son being gay? Were they thinking about kicking him out? Would they do that?

"I feel like shit," Andrew announced as Ryder slipped back into the room.

"Here," Ryder said, holding out one steaming mug, holding one for himself in his free hand. "This will make you feel less like it." He grinned faintly.

Andrew took a sip. "This isn't so bad," he said, surprised.

"See? I told you. It has mint in it. My aunt likes it."

"When are they going to be home?"

"I don't know. Soon? It doesn't matter; they won't mind that you're here. We don't have to say anything until tomorrow, though, if you want. It might be easier, so you have some time to think."

Andrew nodded and continued to sip the tea, staring into the flames of the fire. "I'm going to have to face Andrea eventually," he sighed. "I want my room finished. I can't sleep in there with her anymore."

"Understandable. You shouldn't have been sleeping in there to begin with. Your room should have been finished long ago."

"Yeah. But she and I have always been so close, you know? We shared everything: secrets, friends, soccer. A room didn't seem like that big a problem temporarily. Do you know what she called me tonight?"

"No, but I can guess."

"A fag."

"I guessed right," Ryder admitted.

"I didn't think that could hurt, being directed at me. I mean, the guys on the team say it all the time, and it's always been a joke. They don't really mean it."

"Names are different when people say them and really mean them. And when it's directed at you like that."

"I wonder if this is how Joshua feels when people call him that. God, it's awful."

Ryder smiled and patted his shoulder. "Makes everything different, doesn't it? You know, Josh isn't such a bad guy. He's really nice."

"You really did talk to him?"

"Huh? Yeah, I did. Why? You knew about that?"

"Well, Charlie said…back before you and Charlie made up, he said that you were talking to Josh. And he asked if you were…"

"If I was gay? A fag?"

"Yeah. But I said no. Even though I knew, because I didn't want him to say anything to anyone else and cause trouble for you."

"Thanks for that. But knowing your sister it will be out now, no matter what we want. Why don't we just head to bed? You must be exhausted," Ryder said, taking the mug from Andrew's hands.

"How come you're not?"

"I wasn't the one to face the barrage of insults from family. I'll probably be tired after dealing with it at school, if this gets out of control."

If this gets out of control? More like *when*, Andrew thought in despair.

With the mugs in the sink, they headed upstairs. Andrew changed into a pair of Ryder's sweats and crawled into bed with him. At Andrew's insistence, Ryder had locked the door. Once in bed, Ryder pulled him close and kissed his forehead. "Just get some sleep. Try not to think about it. We'll do that tomorrow."

Andrew nodded and closed his eyes. He felt Ryder fall asleep next to him, but it didn't come so easily for him. Andrew lay awake a long time, staring up at the ceiling, thinking about what the morning would bring. Would his sister be rational and apologize for what she said? Would his parents even want to see him? What would Charlie and Sarah say when they found out?

CHAPTER TWENTY-TWO

A ndrew woke the next morning to an empty bed. He rolled over and looked at the clock, which told him he had slept until after ten. He'd barely gotten any sleep last night. Groaning, he sat up and rubbed his eyes. Somewhere in the house he could hear voices. One of them must have been Ryder.

He got up out of bed and grabbed some of Ryder's clothes and tugged them on. His own jeans were suspiciously missing. Hesitating at the door, he finally opened it and went downstairs.

Ryder and his aunt and uncle sat in the living room, all nursing cups of coffee. When they saw him come into the room, Mrs. Kensington smiled and stood up. "Morning, Andrew. There's breakfast in the kitchen if you want it. You'll have to heat it up, though."

"Thanks," he replied, though food didn't entice him. Instead he got a cup of coffee and joined them in the living room. He took a sip before setting it on the table. "So, Andrew, Ryder tells us you had a bit of trouble last night," Mr. Kensington said softly to break the tension. It only served to make it worse.

"You could say that, yeah."

"We just want you to know that if you need to stay here for a few days until things smooth over, then that's fine with us. And if you'd like, I'll talk with your father."

"Thank you, Mr. Kensington, but I don't know how they would take that."

"Sure. I know it's none of my business."

After a few minutes of tense silence, Ryder's uncle cleared his throat, sipped his coffee and straightened up. "You should give your parents a call. They're probably worried about you."

"They would have called by now if they really were," Andrew argued, but he knew he had a point. His stomach knotted at the prospect of calling, and he took a sip of his coffee to stall the moment, though it tasted like ash in his mouth.

Andrew left to make the call, standing outside of the living room but close enough for help should his father, say, climb through the phone to kill him. He dialed the number as slowly as possible, taking a deep breath to steady himself as he pressed the last button and waited. Temptation to press the End Call button pulsed through his veins.

He prayed his sister didn't answer the phone, but didn't know which would be worse: his father or his mother. The phone continued to ring and he had been about to hang up, relieved and convinced it was a lost cause, when his father answered.

"Hello?"

Andrew took a deep breath, closed his eyes, and leaned against the wall for support. "Dad, it's me."

"Andrew! Thank God you're all right. We thought something happened to you when you wouldn't answer your cell phone."

"I never heard it. Sorry," he said, wondering where he had put his phone. It must have fallen out in the truck.

"Where are you?"

"At the Kensingtons'."

"Thank God. That's what we figured."

"Why didn't you call then?"

"We didn't want to worry them if you hadn't shown up there, Andy. The last thing we wanted was for them to go out to find you and get hurt. I knew I could trust your judgment, even if you left in a hurry last night."

"Dad, I'm sorry. For not telling you a-and for how you found out."

"So it really is true, then?"

Andrew hesitated and stared at the fireplace. The fire burned, though not as brightly as the night before. Maybe the light outside had brightened and made the room glow differently. He paced to the front window and peered out into the near whiteout conditions. Had he really driven through that?

"Andy?"

"Sorry, Dad. Just thinking. Yeah, it really is true. I...really like Ryder. I'm sorry, I know you probably don't want to hear that and you probably think it's horrible and all sorts of—"

"Andy, take a breath. It's all right," said his father, softly. Andrew blinked and pulled back to stare at the phone before listening again. "I'll admit that the news...came as a shock. A big shock, really. But I'm not disgusted."

"You're not? Really? But...what about Mom?"

"Your mother overreacted. I admit it. It caught her by surprise, too. That's just how she chose to express it."

"I'm a disappointment, aren't I?" Andrew asked quietly.

"Why would you say that?"

"Because...I don't know," Andrew said, shrugging though no one could see it.

"Andy, you're not a disappointment, and you never will be. You're a good son, a good kid, and a good student. Your mother loves you, and so do I. But let's have this conversation in person, okay?"

"Okay. Thanks, Dad."

"You're welcome."

"Um...how's Andrea?"

"Andrea is..." His father sighed through the line. "Your sister is another story. I don't know why this has upset her so much. I really can't even begin to guess. We didn't raise either of you with these kinds of prejudices. But you'll have to talk to her about it. That's not something I can speak about for her."

"Okay. And Dad?"

"Yeah?"

"I really, really need my room finished."

His father laughed at that and Andrew managed a small smile. "Believe me, I'm working on it. You'll have it soon. In fact…" He paused and Andrew heard some muffled discussion in the background. Andrew waited and looked behind him to see Ryder watching him intently from his seat in the living room. He gave him a small smile to show he was all right.

"Can you put Kyle on the phone, please? I'd like to talk to him for a moment," he said when he spoke again. Andrew nodded and held out the phone.

"Mr. Kensington, Dad wants to talk to you."

Ryder's uncle took the phone. "Happy New Year, Jack. How are you? Oh, I'm fine," he said, and walked into the other room, just out of earshot.

Andrew sat back down and rested his forehead against his hands. "God, I thought my heart was going to pound out of my chest waiting for him to answer, and then when he finally did, ugh."

"Hey, but everything is okay, right? He's not going to like, kick you out or anything, is he?"

"No. He's going to finish my room. I told him I needed my own and he agreed."

Ryder nudged him. "See? It's going to be okay."

Mr. Kensington came back in a few minutes later and hung up the phone. "I just talked to your father and we worked something out. From what I understand, your sister is the one who let your secret slip, right?"

Andrew nodded.

"And you share a room with her?"

He nodded again.

"That's probably not going to be the best idea right now, you two having to go back to sharing a room. Your father and I agreed that you both need some time to cool down. And since we're such good friends and I'm such a great guy," he said with a wink, "we agreed that it would be the best for everyone if you came to stay here until your father finishes your room."

Andrew stared up at him in surprise. "Really?"

"Really."

Ryder grinned widely. "You're the best, Uncle Kyle."

"I know. Anyway, let's go. We're all going to go over there and you can get some things while Lisa and I talk to your parents."

Ryder ran upstairs to get his boots. Andrew followed him up and Mr. Kensington went outside to clean off the truck. In his room, Ryder laced up his thick winter boots and grabbed gloves.

"This is going to be great. We can go riding all the time if you're staying here!" he said, excitement clear on his face. It was evident that, at least for the moment, he'd forgotten the reason why Andrew would be staying with them. He nodded and smiled a bit. "What's wrong?" Ryder asked when Andrew didn't respond with the same enthusiasm.

"It'll be great, yeah, but there's still my sister. And when we go back to school, what's she going to say? And not only that, won't you get sick of seeing me all the time like that? I mean…"

Andrew trailed off and Ryder stood up. He tugged his face up to look at him and gave him a gentle smile that melted Andrew's heart. "I'm not going to get sick of you. Trust me. I…really care about you," he said, pausing only slightly. "And I don't want to see you upset. Besides, we were friends first, right? No matter what happens, we'll always have that."

No matter what happens? "Right," Andrew said and watched as he bounced out of the room. When Ryder called for him to hurry, Andrew followed, wondering what, if anything, he meant by that.

❖

The ride to his house took a lot longer than normal because of the horrible conditions outside. The snowstorm still raged on and the weatherman on the radio mentioned the possibility of it worsening. If the conditions held as they were, a blizzard would be inevitable. All they needed were higher winds.

Ryder's aunt and uncle talked to fill the silence. Andrew kept catching Ryder glancing at him as he looked out the window, lost in his thoughts. He wanted to look over and reassure Ryder that he was fine, but he just couldn't. He didn't know if he was fine. Everything seemed up in the air.

When they arrived at his house, the driveway had been plowed out, though a fresh coating of snow covered the ground. Mr. Kensington got out of the truck and let the boys out of the back as Andrew's father walked out to meet them.

"Kyle, good to see you," he said and shook his hand. The other man nodded.

"Likewise."

"How are the roads?"

"A little slick, but we were fine. Can't say the same for a few of the cars we passed. Tow trucks are making some good money today."

His father chuckled and nodded. "I hear that." When he saw Andrew, his face sobered. Andrew braced himself for anything, but was surprised when his dad pulled him into a hug. "Don't ever scare me like that again, okay? Going out in a storm like this and driving like a bat out of hell."

"I'm sorry, Dad," Andrew said, choking up.

"Let's go inside. Your mother made coffee for everyone."

The five of them went into the warm house, took off their jackets, and stomped the snow off their boots. Andrew looked around for his sister but couldn't find her.

"She's in our room, watching TV. We told her to stay there until you got your things," his father said and nodded to the stairs. "Go on up and get your stuff, then come down and talk with us, okay?"

Andrew nodded and Ryder followed him up the stairs. He could hear the television in his parents' room and hesitated by the door, but Ryder pushed him forward.

Together they packed a bag with a bunch of his jeans and shirts and threw in his new sneakers. As an afterthought, Andrew grabbed his book bag as well and shouldered it.

"That's all you want to take?" Ryder asked, looking around the room.

Andrew shrugged. "I can always come back if I need something."

"True," acknowledged Ryder, and took the other bag. Andrew once again hesitated outside his parents' door but Ryder pushed him on. "She's not ready yet, Andy. Just keep going."

Andrew stopped in the bathroom quickly to grab a few things before they went back downstairs. His parents and Ryder's aunt and uncle were in the kitchen sipping coffee when they entered. They placed the bags by the door with their coats. His mother looked up from her coffee and stared at her son, and Andrew got the feeling she saw him in a way she never had before. He looked away from her, unable to hold her gaze.

"Ready?" Mr. Kensington asked, and he nodded. "We were just working out a time frame."

"I think we can have your room ready in a week, Andy."

"Thanks, Dad." Andrew looked up at his mother when she didn't say anything and hesitated. It seemed like all he did recently was hesitate. "Mom, I'm really sorry," he started, but couldn't finish. He didn't know what the "sorry" was for. *Sorry that I ran out last night and worried them? Sorry for upsetting her? Sorry for liking Ryder? Sorry for finding who I really am and acting on it? I'm not sorry for that.*

"Listen to what Mr. and Mrs. Kensington say. Make sure you help out when they ask you to. They're doing you a big favor by letting you stay there," she said, nodding toward them.

A lump rose in Andrew's throat. He just wanted his mom to say everything was okay. "I know, and I appreciate it."

They all stood and Andrew waited awkwardly by the door with Ryder. He'd never felt more uncomfortable in his own house than he did at that moment. After they had all pulled on their jackets, his father gave him a pat on the shoulder.

"If you want to come home early, just let us know. We'll figure something out. And just because you're staying there doesn't mean you can't come over or call, okay?"

"I know. Thanks, Dad."

His mother stepped up to him and stared at him for a moment

before giving him a brief hug. "Don't cause any trouble." She glanced at Ryder and nodded.

"He can't get in much out there, Mrs. Morris."

Andrew watched his mother nod at Ryder, then look away.

Ryder helped him stow his things in the back and they climbed in. When they pulled out of the driveway and started back for the farm, Andrew looked up. In his parents' bedroom window he saw the figure of his sister watching him. As soon as she noticed him looking, she pulled back. He sighed.

"Give her time," Mrs. Kensington said. "Change is hard to accept for some people. Especially when they think they know the other person better."

"Yeah, you're right. Thank you," Andrew said, hoping what she said was true.

CHAPTER TWENTY-THREE

It took Ryder's uncle over an hour to drive back to the farm. The roads were worse than they had been before and even the truck, with its four-wheel drive, slid on the slick surface. The plows were struggling to keep up with the snowfall, and with the wind blowing it around, visibility nearly reached zero.

In the backseat, Ryder discreetly held on to Andrew's hand; his thumb rubbed slow circles over the back of it. Andrew looked at the whiteout conditions outside the window and made a face.

"We're going to have to turn the heat up in the barn," his aunt said. "And get out the heavier blankets in case we let the horses out."

"Blankets are in the storeroom. It won't be that difficult."

"What a way to ring in the New Year, huh?" Ryder asked, amazed. "Never seen so much snow in my life."

"Just wait, Tex. This is nothing. It's just the first of the good storms, and it'll only get worse as the winter wears on," his uncle said.

Andrew nodded, forcing himself to join in on the conversation despite his head being filled with worry. "One winter we had ten feet of snow from just one storm."

"One storm?" asked Ryder, amazed. "That's crazy."

"Yeah, they call that the 'lake effect.' It comes from the Great Lakes. We had, like, five inches of snow an hour." Lots of things could change in an hour...

"Wow," Ryder managed to say as he stared out the window, stunned.

They arrived safely, surprised and relieved to find the driveway had been plowed out. "Have to call Carl and see if he did that," Mr. Kensington said as he parked. "Thank him for it."

Andrew grabbed his bags and followed them inside. He followed Ryder up the stairs and walked into his room to set his bags down when he felt a hand on the back of his shirt tugging him out. Mrs. Kensington smiled and shook her head. "I don't mind you two dating, and you're more than welcome to stay here, but I don't want you two staying together in the same room," she said, and motioned for him to move down the hall.

"Oh," Andrew said, startled. His face heated. "I didn't even think."

"It's okay." She stopped at the next door over and opened it. The plain room held a twin bed and dresser. The walls had been painted in brown tones, and the single window looked out over the fields. Embarrassment must've shown on his face.

Lisa softened her tone. "It would be the same if either of you had been a girl, okay? You boys are in high school."

Andrew nodded. "No, I understand. The room's great. Thank you."

She smiled and turned the heat up. "It'll be warm in here before you go to bed tonight. But the thermostat is right here if you need to adjust it either way. You and Ryder can share the bathroom down the hall."

"Okay."

"Take your time settling in." She left him alone after that and Andrew unpacked his bags with a heavy heart.

When he looked up ten minutes later, Ryder stood in the doorway, grinning. Andrew could read the lust in his eyes and he backed up.

"Oh no. We're not. Not with your aunt and uncle home," he warned.

"I know that, but when they're out…" Ryder winked.

"Which they're not going to be. Have you seen the storm?"

Andrew gestured toward the window and Ryder nodded, crossing the small distance to peer out the blinds.

"Yeah, it's just crazy. You can hardly see anything out there. Definitely can't go riding in that. It's dangerous." He crossed his arms and leaned one shoulder against the wall. "What exactly do y'all do when there's blizzards and stuff?"

"Watch TV or movies, read. I don't know. We just entertain ourselves." He shrugged.

"Well, we could always get that homework out of the way so we can spend any better weather outside."

"Much as I really don't want to do that, it's probably a good idea."

"Told you I was smart."

The boys had their books spread out on the floor of the living room in front of the fireplace and lay on their stomachs side by side to work on it. Andrew had just finished a short essay on *Heart of Darkness* when Mrs. Kensington walked in from the barn. The cold air flowed quickly through the house to chill the boys and sent loose papers flying.

"Hey!" Ryder yelled and slapped a hand down on an escaping sheet of loose leaf.

"Sorry, boys. It's freezing out there. Looks like it's going to be a rough night. We put an old stable blanket on Cobalt, Ryder. That should keep him more comfortable."

"Thanks, Aunt Lisa."

"I'm going to make something to drink," she announced before leaving them alone. "Hot chocolate sound good?"

"Sounds great," Ryder said, looking toward Andrew, who added, "Thank you."

Ryder turned back to his homework, but Andrew let his mind wander to this craziness with Andrea. Of all the people in the world, he never expected his sister to turn away from him. It hurt—that was the biggest thing.

After Ryder's aunt dropped off two steaming mugs of hot chocolate and left the room, Andrew glanced over at Ryder, who was blowing steam off the top of his mug.

"Ryder?"

Ryder lifted an eyebrow in question.

"Do you think my sister will tell anyone at school?"

"If she's still really angry about it, probably. I think she'll definitely tell Sarah and Charlie. And if they know…" Ryder let the rest of his sentence hang unspoken in the air.

"Damnit, I'm sorry."

"It's all right. I don't mind. It was bound to happen eventually."

"But do you really want to…you know…"

"Come out?" Ryder shrugged and sat up. He leaned his back against the couch and tucked his legs against him. "To be honest, I'd thought about it. And I don't know which would be harder, in or out. I mean, I know what it's like now. But at least with being out, I wouldn't have to make things up about who I'm interested in or why I didn't just go for it with some girl, or any of that other bullshit. And I'm really getting tired of lying." He studied the marshmallows floating on his cocoa for a few moments, then looked back at Andrew. "I think it'd be fine for me. What other people think about me is beginning to matter less and less. What about you?"

"I don't know. I think it'll be really hard. Soccer is over for the year, so I wouldn't have to go back to that. But still." He paused. "I know just about everyone in the school. News like this is going to get around fast. And, you know, they don't treat Josh with much respect. I don't want that to happen to me. To us."

"Maybe it'll be different with us. Who knows? We might find out no one cares."

"Andrea does. Charlie will."

"Then is he really a friend? If he's going to treat you like shit, then I think he's an awful friend. If he's willing to throw away years of friendship over something that doesn't even concern him, he's not worth it."

Andrew cut his glance away.

"I'm sorry for saying it, but it's true."

"No, you're right." Andrew sat up and sighed, rubbing a hand over his face. He looked sheepishly at Ryder. "Even if everyone finds out, I'm not going to be comfortable holding hands in school or anything like that."

"I would never ask you to. I'm all for affection, but not in public. My personal life is private. No one needs visual proof that we're together."

"Exactly."

"I hate it when straight couples do that. It's like they're trying to prove something. Like ownership of the other, you know?" He made a face.

"You're a lot easier than a girl," Andrew said dryly.

"I should hope so!" Ryder laughed.

Andrew drained the rest of his hot chocolate, then managed to finish his essay without thinking too much about the other kids at school. He still had a few days left before they went back, and he couldn't do anything about it at the moment. Before they returned to school, he would go home and talk to Andrea. Maybe his parents would have talked to her by then, and she would be calmer. Maybe this whole thing would just blow over and he could go home and act like nothing ever happened. Maybe he'd be able to come out on his own, when he and Ryder were really ready.

That is a whole lot of maybes, he grimly realized.

Life was turning out to be a whole lot of maybes...

CHAPTER TWENTY-FOUR

A ndrea, please," Andrew begged, standing at the door. It was the night before school started again. The blizzard had faded out and left a mess of snow, but plows had cleared the roads and school started again on the fourth. He'd come home with the hopes of talking to Andrea, but she wouldn't listen.

"I'm not keeping your dirty little secret for you, Andrew."

Frustration flared. It wasn't a dirty little anything. It was Andrew—who he was. "Why are you so angry about this?" No answer. "Is it because I didn't tell you?" Still nothing. "Listen, I'm sorry, but I didn't want anyone to know. Not even you. You have to understand that. Even if you don't like that, you have to respect it."

Their bedroom door flew open, and Andrea came nose to nose with him. "You, talking about respect? I've never kept anything from you!" she screamed. "I'm not just one of the kids at school. I'm your sister!" Andrew flicked a glance toward the stairs. He knew his parents were down there, listening. Over the phone before he'd come, his parents had said they tried talking to her, but she was being as stubborn as usual when things were out of her control. Andrew hoped that's all it was.

"Why is my being gay so hard for you to accept?" he asked, softly.

"Because it's just not right! I-it's wrong!" she stammered, face getting red.

"Why do you think it's wrong?" he asked. Maybe the gentle approach would work? Desperation filled him at this point. Half an hour of listening to her scream at him through a door had gotten them nowhere. "I don't understand, Andy. You're my sister, like you said. My twin."

"Because all this time you've dated girls and told me all these things. You've *lied* to me all along!"

"I didn't lie! I didn't even know, okay? Yeah, I dated girls. I just thought I got bored quickly. I didn't know why until—"

"Until Ryder showed up and ruined everything. I wish he'd go back to Texas. Better yet, I wish he had never come. Suddenly you don't even want to go to college together anymore? And you don't want to play soccer? It's his fault—"

"No, it isn't." Andrew stepped closer to her. "Don't blame this on him. Yes, he helped me figure things out about myself, but not about soccer."

Andrea growled in frustration and paced back and forth in the hall.

Andrew spread his arms wide. "Whether you believe it or not, this would have happened sooner or later. Maybe not this year, maybe not next, but I would have figured it out eventually." He softened his tone. "I'm gay, Andrea. Nothing's going to change that. I can't help it if it's part of who I am." He paused. Swallowed. "And being gay, meeting Ryder…none of that had anything to do with my decision on choosing Utica over UConn."

Her eyes narrowed, hands in fists by her legs. "How did you get so comfortable saying that so fast? 'I'm gay,' like it's just… nothing."

"It's not nothing, but I'm not ashamed of it."

"How long have you known?"

"Two months."

"Two *months*?" she spat. "You've been dating girls for years and you suddenly change and say you're different because of two *months*? How do you know this isn't just an experiment and you'll go back to liking girls?"

He lowered his tone to a whisper. "Who are you, Mom? This isn't an experiment, Andrea."

"But how do you know?"

"How do *you* know you like guys?"

She pressed her lips together, searched his eyes.

"I'm sorry if you don't like it, if you can't find it within you to understand." A pause. "You don't have to. But this is who I am. I'm your brother, and I'm gay."

Emotion reddened Andrea's face. "You're going to have to face the consequences of your choice, Andrew."

He was just tired. "This isn't a choice. And what are you going to do? Tell the whole school?"

"Maybe."

"Go right ahead then, Andrea, but think about it. What is that going to accomplish, huh? Soccer is over. School gets out in less than six months. I'll deal with whatever gets thrown at me until then." He sounded confident to his own ears, but inside he felt his stomach start to churn.

"Are you really ready to do that? You really think you can handle going from Mr. Popular to the one everyone talks about because he's sleeping with a guy?"

Andrew's stomach clenched, but he kept his chin lifted.

"You think you can handle being another Joshua Grayson?" Andrea asked, crossing her arms over her chest.

"I think I'd rather handle being myself than pretending I'm something I'm not. There's nothing wrong with Joshua Grayson."

"Whatever you say," she said, in a skeptical tone.

"You know what? I'm not talking to you when you're like this. I've said my piece, you've said yours. I'm leaving. If you want to talk like a rational person, like the sister I thought you were, you know where you can reach me."

"Fine, leave. Walk away—"

"I will, and I'll only say one last thing: Don't do something that you're going to regret in the end. There are some things you can say and do that you'll never be able to take back, no matter how sorry you are later."

Andrew left without another word. He shook his head toward his parents before leaving the house and getting in the truck to drive back to the Kensington farm. Ryder had wanted to come along this time, to try to help talk to her, but Andrew had said no; he thought it would only exacerbate the situation. After this meeting, he thought the only way it could have been worse was if she had decided to throw a punch.

So much for a twin bond.

While he drove back, he thought about everything that had happened in the last two, almost three months. He'd broken up with not one, but two girlfriends, found out he liked guys—no, not any guy, Ryder—and started dating again. He'd gotten into fights with friends he'd never fought with before, but made a new one and strengthened other friendships. He'd also learned he knew very little about his sister.

The sister he thought he knew was open and accepting and sweet despite her headstrong and driven ways. The headstrong part still existed, that was for sure. But she also appeared to be vicious, controlling, and more close-minded than she let others believe. She'd gone behind his back and applied for UConn for the both of them. She refused to let him make his own decisions about his life and wanted to control every aspect of his. Now this.

Sure, there were things about him that had changed. But as far as he was concerned, they were all good things. They made him a better person. *Ryder* made him a better person. If Andrea couldn't see that, it was her loss.

Andrew kept telling himself that when he pulled into the driveway and climbed out of the truck. He heard voices from the barn and went to check it out.

Most of the horses were out in one of the cleared fields, running through the light covering of snow that remained on the ground. The only one left in his stall was Dante.

"How'd it go?" Mr. Kensington asked.

Andrew shrugged.

"That bad, huh?" Ryder asked.

He wanted to focus on horses now, not on Andrea. He lifted his chin toward Dante. "He looks particularly mean today." Andrew looked meaningfully at Ryder, who sat on the stall door, trying to coax the horse forward with a carrot. The horse refused to budge.

"He doesn't want to go out. I don't think he likes the snow," Ryder said, letting the conversation about Andrea go.

"So, can't he stay inside?"

"He needs exercise. And we should be working with him every day," Mr. Kensington said. "I'm sorry about your sister, son."

Ryder nodded.

"I'm surprised she didn't punch me," Andrew muttered ruefully. "It got really loud for a while, but my parents didn't step in."

"Believe me, it's better they didn't. From the sound of it, your sister would have forced them to pick sides. That would be messy for everyone. It's best they let the two of you have it out," Mr. Kensington said.

"God, this is such a mess. I told her before I left not to do anything she'd regret, you know? Because there are some things that I wouldn't be able to forgive if she said."

Mr. Kensington leaned back against the wall and tilted his head. "She's your sister. Don't you think you'd forgive her eventually?"

"I don't know. Maybe. But at the same time, if she says anything really bad against me, it's always going to be there."

"What is it she could say that would get you that upset?" he asked, curious.

"Spread rumors about me, lies. Tell everyone every detail they don't need to know. The really embarrassing things."

"Well, keep in mind she is your sister, like it or not at the moment. She might be hurting right now, but I'm sure she still loves you. And if she says anything, she's probably just lashing out. It'll pass. Things always do." He gave Andrew a squeeze on his shoulder, before stepping past them to head to his office.

Andrew leaned up against the wall where Ryder sat, and soon felt fingers playing in his hair. He glanced up. "It really sucked," he said.

"No matter what, we'll get through this," Ryder said softly, reassuringly.

Andrew wanted to believe him, but his heart and mind were conflicted. Sure, they'd get through it. But would they get through it intact?

CHAPTER TWENTY-FIVE

Andrew wasn't sure what he had expected at school that Thursday morning classes resumed, but it wasn't this. He had pulled into the parking lot with Ryder and gotten out of the car. He didn't know if Andrea had arrived yet, though he suspected she had. She would have wanted to get a head start on her schemes.

Expecting to be cornered and questioned mercilessly by friends and teammates, Andrew felt surprised yet relieved when he made it first to the school door unscathed, and then to his locker. And after that, first-period class.

With a sigh he sat down, thinking perhaps he'd been too dramatic, making everything seem worse than it really was.

Ryder joined him a short time later and gave him a small smile. He leaned over and put his hand on the back of his seat like he did nearly every morning since he'd arrived. "Anything?"

"Nothing. I guess I overreacted. It's going to be fine," Andrew said with a sigh of relief.

"That's great," Ryder agreed.

More of the class started to file in and a few greeted them and smiled. With every person who set foot in the room, though, Andrew couldn't help but feel like the bomb was about to drop any second, and he could do nothing but wait. Most of the students, though, looked tired or disappointed to be back—worried about their own lives, not his. One or two asked how his and Ryder's vacations went. Typical post-vacation chatter.

Until Sarah walked in.

Sarah walked into the room with Nathaniel, laughing at something he said. When she turned down the row to take her seat in front of Andrew she paused and gave Nathaniel a knowing look. The expression on his face was a mixture of amusement and disgust, and Andrew's stomach lurched.

Andrea really had told.

"So," Sarah said as she sat down. "Have a good vacation? We didn't get to talk much on New Year's, and you all but disappeared after that party."

"Yeah," Andrew replied, swallowing hard and smiling. "Just great. A little busy, that's all. You?"

"It was fine. I'm sure not as interesting as yours, from what Andrea says."

"Oh yeah? What uh, did Andrea say?"

"She said you had a very eventful New Year and that you're now living with Ryder."

"Just until my room is finished," Andrew clarified. He felt a bead of sweat begin to form at his hairline.

"So that's why you never wanted to go out with me, Ryder? Because you were more into guys?" Sarah asked. Her voice sounded sweet, but a hint of acid tinted it.

Ryder looked over at her and shrugged languidly, his face blank.

Some of the students in front of her heard what she said and turned to each other, whispering excitedly. They looked back at Ryder, trying to figure out what Sarah was talking about.

"That's why you kept rejecting me, isn't it? Because you wanted Andrew and not me, huh?"

"Yeah, Sarah. That's it. Is that what you want me to say? Now just drop it."

Andrew felt his face flame and he hung his head as an excited storm of whispers moved around the room. The second bell rang and Mrs. Appleby walked in. She called the class to order, and when she didn't get it, she slammed a book down on her desk.

"Excuse me. Now, I am well aware that this is the first class on the first day back from vacation. However, we have work to do. In three short weeks, not including this one, you have your midterm." The class erupted in disgruntled noises. "Yes, groan all you want," she added. "But you're still responsible for learning the information. Now take out your texts and notebooks."

The whispers behind her caught Mrs. Appleby's attention. She turned to look, her eyes narrowed in annoyance, assessing the situation. Some of the students were talking in small groups of two or three, though most had listened. Andrew and Ryder sat in stony, uneasy silence, ignoring the whispers and stares. Andrew's pencil rolled off his desk. He leaned down to pick it up.

"Fag," someone murmured.

Mrs. Appleby's hand dropped noisily to her desk. "One more thing," she said keeping her voice low. The students stopped to listen, waiting for something important. "Like you, I still want to be on vacation, and as such, I am not in the mood to tolerate any nonsense today. If I hear one derogatory comment directed toward anyone, for any reason, you are out of here. I don't care if it's a joke, and I don't care if it's 'not meant that way.' I hear it and you have a detention after school tomorrow and a trip to the principal's office immediately. Yes?"

The class nodded, subdued for the moment, and she went back to her teaching. Andrew had never been more grateful for history class in his life. As the rest of the class shuffled about getting their books and notebooks out, he realized Karina's seat was still empty. He had hoped she would be there that morning. She had been so accepting of his relationship with Ryder, he hadn't realized he relied on her support today. Maybe she would turn up before the period ended.

❖

Class ended and Ryder and Andrew had to part for the rest of their classes. Karina didn't make it to class at all, so Andrew was left alone as he waved to Ryder on his way to second period. Each class proceeded like history had, except without Ryder, things seemed a little quieter. No one specifically asked him anything, but he heard the whispers and saw the looks. He avoided them as best he could, but Nathaniel blocked his entrance to fourth-period English.

When Andrew tried to walk around him, Nathaniel sidestepped and blocked him. With an impatient sigh, Andrew looked up at Nathaniel's smirk. He tried to step to the other side and get around him, but Nathaniel pushed forward and knocked him into the lockers.

"Watch where you're walking, faggot."

"Then don't get in my way," Andrew muttered, pushing past him.

Nathaniel gave him another shove with his shoulder, and Andrew grunted from the pressure. It would leave a bruise later.

"You better watch your back," he said as he pinned Andrew to the corner of the locker. The hard metal bit into his back, but he kept his face composed. "You're not always going to have your little boyfriend or friends around to save your sorry ass."

I am not going to let him win.

"I don't see anyone around now, do you? Back off, Nathaniel. You're nothing but talk." Andrew shifted his weight, catching his knee against Nathaniel's. It pushed him off and he managed to slip past him into the doorway next to him.

English class was blissfully empty and Nathaniel didn't follow him. He sat down at his desk and briefly rested his forehead against the cool surface. His shoulder had already started to ache from Nathaniel's force, and he rubbed a hand over it casually. He was about to place his copy of *Heart of Darkness* on his desk when Joshua Grayson sat on its flat surface.

"So. Is it true?" he asked softly.

Andrew got a really good look at him for the first time. Funny how he'd known the boy for four years and had never *really* looked at him. But he did now. Josh had short, wavy, light brown hair that flipped out at the ends. His eyes were a pale hazel, and his nose turned up slightly at the end. "Don't say 'is what true' because I know you know what rumors are going around. It's hard to miss rumors like that. They have the tendency to move the fastest."

"Yeah, it's true," Andrew admitted.

Josh shrugged, one eyebrow quirking up. "Well, never figured you were family. But I guess I didn't really know you either."

"Guess not."

"So, Ryder?"

"Yup."

"He's a nice guy. Talked to me his first day here. Even after that prick Justin Mast told him *all* about me, not that he really knows," he said, rolling his eyes. "Anyway, I just wanted to say ignore all that." He waved a hand. "It can be annoying, yeah, but you build up a tough skin after a while."

"You seem really…cool about it all," Andrew said.

"Let me guess, you thought I would cry about it like the rest of your teammates? Just because of the rumors about me?"

"Well, yeah, no offense."

"None taken," he said with a small, sad smile. "Like I said. You build a tough skin. You either let it roll off and ignore it, or you get eaten alive."

"Thanks for the advice," Andrew said as the bell rang. Josh took his seat. He sat in the front of the room and ignored most of the people who talked to him.

Andrew knew some of the whispers around the room were directed toward him, but he tried to take Josh's advice and ignore it. He didn't look forward to lunch, though, where he'd have to face his sister and friends.

By the time lunch came around his stomach churned, and he wanted to skip it altogether, but he knew he'd have to face it sooner or later. Better to just get it over with all at once. He hoped he'd made the right decision when he walked into the lunchroom and got in line to buy food. No one sat at his usual table, so he took his seat and waited.

Anxiety flooded Andrew's body as he pushed his food around the plate. He ended up pushing it away as he waited for Ryder to join him. Glancing around the cafeteria, he felt like all eyes were on him. Every whisper seemed to be amplified and he bristled with each word.

"Look at him sitting over there. Who knew?"

"Faggot."

"Andy and Ryder? That's sick."

"Charlie was right about Ryder."

"Poor Sarah. She really liked him."

Ryder joined Andrew a minute later carrying his lunch. He took the seat across from him this time, rather than next to, helping Andrew block out everyone else.

"How are you doing?" Ryder asked, concern barely masking the stress on his face. His eyes were narrowed and little lines bunched at the corners.

"I've been better. But not bad, considering," Andrew lied with a furtive glance around the room. "I talked to Josh today in English."

"Nice guy, isn't he?"

Andrew nodded. "He said the same thing about you."

Andrew saw Andrea enter the lunchroom and looked up. He followed her approach across the large, noisy room, straight to their table. His body tensed as she stopped behind Ryder, holding her bag.

Neither of them said anything to each other, and Ryder glanced over his shoulder to look up at her. She kept her face calmly blank, and then turned when she heard her name called from across the room. Sarah stood there, calling her and waving from another table. She pointedly left without a word and Andrew felt both relieved and hurt at the same time.

"You knew it would happen, Andy. Just let it go. It's better than her making a scene, right?"

Andrew mumbled his agreement and picked at his food. They had the table to themselves, and while it would have been fine before, now it felt uncomfortable.

Students still filed into the lunchroom. Most of them were stragglers who had been talking to teachers after class, or who met with their boyfriends and girlfriends in the hallways. Two in particular caught Andrew's attention and made him look up.

Nathaniel and Charlie strode into the cafeteria together, side by side. It took them only a second to spot Andrew and Ryder and Nathaniel's face lit up.

"Oh shit," Andrew groaned and Ryder spun to see what he was looking at.

"Great. Charlie."

"And Nathaniel. I had problems with him earlier, before English class."

"Why didn't you tell me?" Ryder demanded, looking back at him, concerned. Andrew didn't have time to answer.

Near silence fell on the cafeteria as Charlie and Nathaniel stood in front of their table. Andrew glanced over at Andrea's table and caught her eye briefly, but she turned away from him.

"How's it going, boys?" Charlie asked, his face twisted in a sneer. Andrew never thought his friend was the best-looking guy, but his anger had turned him ugly.

"What do you want, Charlie?" Ryder asked, getting straight to the point.

"Just checking in on my two favorite people. I hear you had a great vacation together. Isn't that right, Nate? Got a little cozy at Ryder's place, didn't you, Andrew?" Nathaniel took a seat next to Ryder and Charlie sauntered around the table until he was next to Andrew. He sat casually in the open seat next to him.

Andrew stared at his former friend. "You used to spend the night at my place, Charlie."

"Yeah, well, I'm not a faggot, am I? And that was before I knew you were one. I'd never do that now. Wouldn't want the two of you turning me gay." Nathaniel snickered at his comment and Charlie grinned at him.

"What's going on?"

Andrew turned and saw Karina striding across the cafeteria.

For a moment, all eyes were on her and he breathed a sigh of relief. She joined Ryder and Andrew at the table and rested a hand on Andrew's shoulder.

"Sorry I didn't make it to first period," she said softly.

"No big deal," Andrew replied, trying to ignore Charlie leaning closer to him.

"It's too late to hide what you are, Andy. Everyone knows," Charlie said with a smug look on his face, ignoring Karina. "And I knew you were a queer, Ryder. I knew it when I saw you talking to Josh."

"Just because I talked to him didn't mean anything, Charlie."

"Whatever. Like I said, Andy. Everyone knows you're a fag."

"Back off, Charlie," Ryder warned. "This is none of your business. It wasn't to begin with, but you had to get involved."

All eyes were on them as Charlie stood and leaned over the table, invading Ryder's personal space. Andrew found himself standing and moving quickly to Ryder's side. Nathaniel stood as well.

"I wasn't talking to you, Coltrane. I was talking to your little boyfriend."

Everything moved so quickly. Charlie came around the table just as Ryder's fingers curled into a fist. Charlie mirrored his pose. Andrew stepped between them, shoving Charlie back as he came forward. A fist—Charlie's—connected awkwardly with his already bruised shoulder and then a shout from the other side of the cafeteria.

Andrew turned in time to see Andrea running over. She pushed Charlie and Nathaniel out of the way and stood between them and Andrew.

"What the hell are you doing, Charlie?" she demanded. "You've already done enough."

"Done enough? Andrea, I'm just getting started. It's what you wanted. You wanted me to—"

"I didn't want you to do it like this!" Andrea shouted. "This is just wrong!"

Charlie laughed. "Wrong? You're the one who wanted to make his life miserable. You're the one who told us everything. Every little detail."

The monitors on duty were headed toward them and Ryder pulled Andrew back, but he shrugged him off.

"I never said to do it like this. Leave him alone, Charlie."

"It's too late for that, Andrea." Nathaniel laughed.

Students started talking now, pointing out the scene and discussing it with their friends. Andrew couldn't hear what they said, but it didn't matter anymore.

In front of him, Nathaniel and Charlie laid into Andrea.

It didn't matter anymore that she'd started it. She'd tried to stop it. When he had needed her the most she had come to his defense and told Charlie to back off. Now she needed him.

"Charlie, get lost," he finally said, finding his voice. He stood straighter next to his sister, holding his ground.

Charlie laughed until he saw the look on his face. "What are you going to do, huh? You're—"

"Gay. Yes. You've made it quite clear. Is that what you want to hear? Fine. I'm gay, Charlie. Get over it. Come on, Andrea." Andrew grabbed Andrea's hand and pulled her away from the two of them just as the cafeteria monitors descended on Charlie and Nathaniel. Karina and Ryder were close behind them, and from the corner of Andrew's eye, he saw Melissa get up as well.

❖

Andrea disappeared with an excuse right after they left the lunchroom, leaving Andrew completely speechless. Why was she running off? He needed to talk to her. Find out what had caused her to change her mind and confront Charlie like that.

The boys met at Andrew's truck after school. Andrew had waited for his sister at her locker, but she never showed up.

The drive back to his temporary home was silent. After ten minutes of nothing, Ryder reached over and took his hand. Andrew turned his palm up and they clasped, resting them against the seats.

"I don't get Andrea," Andrew murmured, and Ryder nodded his agreement.

The conversation, or lack thereof, lapsed again until they made it to the farm. After parking the truck in his designated spot, Andrew and Ryder got their bags and went inside. A fire roared in the living room, heating the house pleasantly. They were in the process of stripping off their jackets and shoes when Mr. and Mrs. Kensington walked into the room.

"So, how did it go?" Mr. Kensington asked.

Andrew flopped onto the couch and groaned.

"That bad?" he asked, and the boys nodded.

"Lunch was the worst."

"Why? What happened?"

Andrew and Ryder each gave a rundown of the event from his perspective.

"I have no idea what Andrea was thinking," Andrew concluded, looking to Mr. Kensington for an answer.

"Maybe she came to her senses. I can't really say, but you should talk to her. Given all that happened, though, I'm proud of both of you for sticking out the whole day."

After Mr. Kensington excused himself, Andrew curled up on the couch, letting the heat from the fire close by warm him. He listened to Ryder talking to his aunt and uncle in the other room as he stared into the fire. He let his eyes shut for just a minute, and when he opened them again, he had a blanket over him and the glow from the fire had faded.

Andrew sat up with a start and looked around the room. The sun hung much lower in the sky, throwing shadows across the room. The light had been turned on in the kitchen and he pushed off the blanket to go investigate.

Ryder and his aunt stood at the counter, cutting vegetables and shoving them in a pot. They spoke in low tones and didn't notice when Andrew stopped and stood in the doorway.

"Are you going to tell your parents about this?" Andrew heard her ask, not looking away from the carrots she sliced.

"I'm going to have to eventually, right? They keep asking me who I'm dating. Mom wants to know if 'the girl's from a family she knows.'"

"Why don't you tell them? They're over there. They'll have plenty of time to think about it before they come back."

"Are you kidding? This is my dad we're talking about. He'll flip out."

"Yes, maybe. But flip out over there, while you're here. That might be the best way to do it."

"I don't know."

"How do you feel about Andrew, then? His parents know. They seem like they've come around to it. Do you think it's fair that they know about you and your parents don't know about him?"

"I like him. I really like him a lot. But I doubt he cares about that. It's not like he's going to meet them. At least, not anytime soon. They're not going to just fly out here and be like, 'Hi, son! How are you?' I'm not going to put him through that."

Andrew took a step back and the floor creaked. They looked over at him and for the first time in a long time, Andrew thought he saw Ryder blush. He looked back down at the celery he had been cutting.

"Sleep well?" Mrs. Kensington asked with a pleasant smile.

"Yeah, uh, thanks. For the blanket, I mean. I didn't realize I was so tired."

"You were talking and then you just went out, like a light," Ryder teased once he gathered his composure.

"That's all right. Could you help us with dinner? I need to go ask Kyle something."

"Sure," he said, and took her place.

"When you're finished cutting the carrots, just toss them in the pot. Ryder, add the celery too, and put in some salt and pepper, okay? I'll be back in ten."

The boys agreed and watched her leave.

"She seems to leave at rather convenient times," Andrew noted dryly.

"That's Aunt Lisa. She has a lot of tact. Especially when it comes to things like this."

"Things like what? Like cooking?"

"No, dork. I mean…when she knows someone wants to tell someone else something important."

"Oh." Andrew grabbed another carrot and cut it up slowly. Beside him, Ryder stood silently.

"You heard us talking, didn't you?"

"Yeah," he admitted. "Sorry."

"It's all right, I guess. I meant what I said."

"Which part? You said a lot," Andrew tried to tease, but the words fell short.

"The part where I said I liked you a lot," Ryder admitted, pausing in cutting the celery. He looked at Andrew, his face completely open, and Andrew could see the honesty there.

"I know. I really like you, too. A lot."

"I know we've only been dating for a couple of months, but—"

"You don't have to say anything else, Ryder, I get it."

The two continued to work in silence, cutting more vegetables and adding them to the pot. Ryder added some water while Andrew put in the salt and pepper. When Andrew put the shakers down, Ryder turned.

"But I think I love you," Ryder blurted, face red. He stared at Andrew with wide eyes, as if he couldn't believe he'd said it, and Andrew stared back, his own cheeks heating.

After a tense moment of silence, the two started to laugh. Ryder pulled him into his arms and leaned back against the counter. "Wow. That so didn't come out how I wanted it to, but okay."

"A little fierce there," Andrew teased.

Ryder looked down at him, head tilted to the side, the question burning in his eyes. Andrew could read it there: Did he love him, too? Andrew didn't say anything, just pulled Ryder's face down to his and gave him a small, gentle kiss.

It was answer enough.

CHAPTER TWENTY-SIX

That night, Andrew's father called to speak to him. "Andrea told me what happened in school today. Are you all right?"

"I'm fine," Andrew replied after taking a moment to process what he said. *Andrea told him? Why?* "How's she doing?" Andrew asked.

His father sighed into the phone. "I don't know. Since she got home she seems different. Quieter. She doesn't look as angry as she did before, but aside from telling us what happened during lunch, she won't talk about it."

"Is she there now? Do you think I could talk to her?"

"She went outside a while ago. Look, son. Your room isn't quite finished yet, but we put the new flooring in. If I stay home tomorrow I can get your furniture moved back in and you can come back home."

As much as Andrew liked staying with the Kensingtons, he did want to go home. He missed seeing his parents and listening to their easy banter. He even missed Andrea.

"I don't want you to miss work."

"It's fine," his father said. "I think it's time you come home. Your mother misses you. I miss you. I know despite what she says, Andrea does, too."

Andrew said good-bye to his father and hung up the phone.

"How did it go?" Ryder asked.

Andrew jerked his head up and saw him leaning against the door frame, arms crossed.

"Room is almost done. Dad said he'll stay home tomorrow to put everything back in and I can move back tomorrow."

"Tomorrow? Wow, that's so soon. I kind of hoped you'd be here longer," Ryder said softly.

"Yeah, I know. I don't know how Andrea's going to take it. I mean after today, who knows what she's thinking. Can't imagine what she's going to do when I'm back at home."

"Well, with you back she'll have to face her problems head-on and get over it."

"Maybe." Andrew shrugged.

"It'll be fine."

"But I don't want to leave. I like it here."

"I know, and I like having you here. But hey, we'll still see each other at school. And you can always sleep over and stuff," Ryder said, raising an eyebrow suggestively.

Andrew flushed and waved a hand. "I know, but it's still not the same, you know?"

Ryder nodded and sat down next to him. "I know. We'll figure something out. Don't worry. I'm not going anywhere. I'll still be right here." He leaned forward and gave him a small kiss. When Ryder pulled away, Andrew pulled him back and the two fell onto the bed. Ryder pulled off one of his shoes and aimed it at the partially open door. It hit it squarely with a *thunk* and the door shut.

"Nice shot," Andrew said, impressed.

"Thanks. Now, where were we?"

CHAPTER TWENTY-SEVEN

If you need to get away, you don't even have to call. Just come back, okay?" Ryder reassured him after Andrew had packed all his things the next day after school. He pulled him into a tight hug. Andrew relaxed and nodded. School that day had been tough, and Andrew kept thinking about going home that night. He had known throughout the day that he'd made the right decision, but now that it was actually time to leave, his stomach twisted in knots.

"I'll call you later and let you know how everything is," he told Ryder as calmly as he could manage to sound.

"Okay. I really wish you would let me go with you."

"I know. But I need to do this myself."

Ryder sighed. "I still wish I could go."

Andrew stretched up and gave him a kiss. "I'll be fine. Andrea and I need to work this out. And we're going to, today, whether she likes it or not."

She didn't show up at school today. I wonder what happened.

Ryder playfully ruffled his hair. "Just don't hurt her too much," he teased.

"I promise I won't," Andrew replied, then hesitated. Three little words had been gaining ground in his mind since he had been spending more time with Ryder, and they threatened to spill out now. The same words Ryder had said earlier. "Ryder, I—" he started, but Ryder cut him off.

"I know, Andrew." He grinned and gave him another kiss. "Get going, or I'll convince you to let me come along."

❖

His father met him outside when he parked the truck and walked in with him. The house hadn't changed except for the holiday decorations being packed away. He felt bad for not having been there to help with it, but shrugged the feeling off.

"Everything is all set. We moved all your things in there, but if you want, we can rearrange them to however you want."

"I'm sure it's fine, Dad. Let's just go up."

The two of them went up the narrow stairs with Andrew following his father. Down the hall from his parents' room his door stood open. The hardwood floor looked fantastic. In the center of the room was a dark blue rug to keep him from freezing his feet in the morning if the room was too cold. The walls were the same light blue shade they had been before, but they had been washed. Without any scuffs or marks, the room seemed larger.

His bed stood in the corner where it used to be, the nightstand right next to it below the window. His mother had changed the curtains and put up dark blue ones; they were open onto the frozen driveway below. His low dresser stood next to the door with his television mounted on the wall and DVD player sitting off to the side. Against the other wall stood his desk, with a small desk light and his laptop sitting there, waiting to be turned on. His swivel chair had been tucked in under the desk. Next to that sat a small three-shelf bookcase.

"It's almost too clean in here," Andrew said, wrinkling his nose. "I mean, there's nothing on my desk or dresser."

"Well, you'll have to fix that, won't you? Sorry we didn't get to change the paint, but we can always do that later."

Andrew nodded. "It's okay. And everything's fine the way it is. I don't need to move anything," he said, and tossed his bag on his bed. His father nodded and set the other bag down. "Where's Andrea?"

"She's been hiding out in her room ever since she helped me move everything back in."

Surprised, Andrew looked up his father. "She helped?"

His father nodded with a small smile. "Yes, she did. I didn't ask her, either. She offered. And I think when you talk to her you'll find she's a little more…reasonable."

Andrew looked up in surprise again. "Did you talk to her?"

"Your mother and I did, yes. We sat down with her and we all talked about you coming home. I think it did a bit of good for her. She's behaving a little more like herself than she has been the last few weeks."

"That's a relief to hear."

"Just go easy on her. This hasn't been easy for her. I know," he said, holding up his hand to cut Andrew off. "I know it's not easy for you, either. And I'm aware it's not right what she did. But think of how your sister feels too, okay? Just think about it. Dinner will be ready soon."

He left a moment later and Andrew sat down on the edge of his bed, alone. The heater in the bedroom had been turned on, so it was comfortably warm, but not as warm as Ryder's had been, and he missed it already. He stood to turn up the thermostat and then sat back down again. A minute later he tore through his bag, sorting clothes to wash. Restless energy filled him. Andrea was just down the hall and he needed to talk to her, but he stalled for time as he tried to collect his thoughts. He wanted to talk before dinner, but he knew waiting until afterward would be better in the long run. But what would he say to her?

❖

Andrea came out of her room after their father's third call up to her. While Mom pulled the roast out of the oven and cut it, the two of them sat in awkward silence: Andrew tapping his fingers on the table, Andrea fidgeting nervously.

By the time the roast was cut and ready to eat, Andrew felt sick. He poked idly at his food, only taking a few bites. Andrea barely touched hers as well. The normal banter that filled the dinner table was absent and a pervasive silence filled the air.

"I'm sorry," Andrew and Andrea said, suddenly and simultaneously, both trying to break the tension. They stared at each other from across the table for a moment and then burst out laughing. It took only that second for the tension to dissipate, and their parents smiled with relief.

The two of them ate quickly and cleared their plates. Without saying a word to each other, they both put on their boots, jackets, and gloves and went outside.

The sun had already set, but the moon in the cloudless sky reflected off the snow, making it bright enough to see. They trudged up the hill through the drifts, heading toward the quiet of the barn. The only sound Andrew could hear came from their boots tramping down a path and the soft puffs of their breath. Everything else was muffled from the snow.

Andrew stopped in front of the pond and looked at the covered surface. Ice had frozen it over and the snow built up on top of it. There were a few spots where animals must have stepped on it and broken through because nothing obstructed the view of the black, frigid water. The trees were completely bare and offered a clear view of the sky above them. When the twins walked to the other edge of the pond, they stopped and stared at the pile of lumber lying beneath a tree. Most of it had been buried under drifts of snow, but pieces of it were poking through.

"It came down," Andrew said, surprise and disappointment in his voice.

"Yeah. Dad thinks it was the storm on New Year's Eve that did it," she said, digging a hole in the snow with her boot. "We thought we heard something outside but he didn't bother to check until he came up a few days later to get something out of the barn."

"Oh. I always hoped we'd fix it up, you know?" Andrew said softly.

"Yeah, but we outgrew that a long time ago. We don't have time for games like that anymore. Even if we had fixed it and made it stronger, it wouldn't have been big enough for the two of us."

"Funny, it seemed bigger than that when we were kids."

"Everything seems bigger when you're a kid," Andrea said

quietly. They stared at the pile for a length of time, standing in silence. Andrew remembered how they had wanted to sleep out there one time when they were nine, and their mother said no. Their father talked her into it, saying they would be fine in the tree. The twins hadn't made it more than five minutes before they scrambled down and begged to come back inside. Andrew smiled at the memory and laughed softly.

"What?" Andrea asked, turning to look at him.

Andrew recalled the memory to Andrea and asked, "Do you think Dad said yes because he knew we wouldn't last out here by ourselves?"

Andrea thought about it for a moment, looking up at the sky. "Hmm…you know, you're probably right."

They shared a laugh and then turned to find the log they often used as a bench. The snow covered it and Andrew had to brush it off before they sat down. It was cold even through his jeans, and Andrea huddled against him to keep warmer.

"So…you're really serious about Ryder?" Andrea finally asked as they stared down at their house.

Andrew could see the lights on in nearly every room downstairs and the glow from the fire. Smoke poured out of the chimney, curling up into the sky before it dissipated. "Yeah, I am."

"And you like him a lot?"

Andrew nodded. "A lot."

"And…he likes you, too?"

"Of course."

"The same amount?" she asked.

"Andrea…"

"Just answer the question."

Andrew sighed, exasperated, and answered, "Yes, the same amount."

"What's it like? Being with him? How did you know?"

"I don't know," Andrew replied. "It just happened. I guess when I started hanging out with him more. I just felt…different around him. And every time I looked at him I got all nervous and jittery. When he came out to me, it didn't seem so bad. Then one day..." Andrew shrugged, not sure of how much to tell her or how she would react to it. It felt weird to have gone from fighting to talking about personal details.

"One day what?"

"One day he asked me if I'd ever kissed a guy before, and when I said no, he kissed me. I wasn't disgusted at all. It felt...right. I don't know how else to say it. It just felt like something that was supposed to happen."

"So what, you were dating right after that?" Andrea asked.

Andrew chuckled. "God, no. I had to think about it for a while. It was good, yeah, but I was scared as hell. Look, Andrea, it's not like I *wanted* to be gay. No one in their right mind would want to face what I have. But I am. I realize that now. I can't change that. And I guess...I don't want to change that. I like the person I've become."

"Couldn't you like...try? You know, just to see?"

"Andrea," he said, looking at her with a warning in his eyes.

She sighed. "All right, I know. I won't say it again. I just wanted to check."

"I really like Ryder, and he likes me, too. And I'm happy for once. I don't have to fake anything because of who I'm dating. Nothing is fake with Ryder, and that's what I love the most. I don't have to pretend anymore. I get to be myself, and so can he."

"When you put it that way, it's hard not to be happy for you," she said softly, reaching down to draw idly in the snow with a gloved hand. Andrew smiled.

"Thanks."

"You're welcome."

"Can I ask you something?" Andrew asked. Andrea nodded and he continued. "In the cafeteria yesterday. What made you stand up to Charlie?"

Andrea reached down and grabbed a handful of snow, and compacted it into a ball before crushing it. "Going after you like that, there, was wrong. I never meant for it to get that bad. When I saw him with Nathaniel, and then heard him, I knew there was going to be trouble. And I couldn't let him do that to you. I'm sorry I even let it get that far."

"I appreciate what you did. Really." He smiled at her and gave her a small nudge. "I think we work better as a team."

Andrea smiled and murmured her agreement.

"And with that out of the way..." Andrew started, looking pointedly at his sister.

She bit her lip and looked down the hill toward the house. "Do we need to have the college conversation?"

"Yes."

Andrea sighed and brushed snow off her gloves. "I'm sorry I forged your application to UConn. I know it wasn't the right thing to do, but we've always said we would go to the same college."

"Things change. UConn isn't what I want."

"Don't you like soccer anymore?"

"I do," Andrew replied softly. "But it's not what I want to do for the rest of my life. I want to concentrate on my education, not sports."

"Don't you want to go to school together?"

Andrew hesitated and contemplated the question. "It's not like I chose another school to get away from you. They offer more of what I'm looking for. And it's not like we're always going to be together, you know?"

"I thought we always would," she admitted.

"Andrea, we'll always be siblings," he said, nudging her gently with his shoulder. "Nothing's going to change that. We'll always be close. But...I think it's time we start finding our own ways."

"I wish we'd wait until after college. Going to UConn without you...is going to be hard. I'll miss you," she admitted and wiped a glove across her eyes. She sniffed, and Andrew wasn't sure if it came from the cold or tears. He reached out and wrapped an arm around her shoulders.

"Hey, college is supposed to be an adventure, right? Think about how much we'll have to tell each other when we're on break.

And it's not like we're going to be across the country! We can visit each other on weekends if we really want to."

"You think?"

"I know it."

Andrea sighed softly and leaned into his arm. He gave her a small hug and rested his head against her soft hair. It would be strange to be at school without her. But it was better for both of them.

"I'll call UConn tomorrow and withdraw my application," Andrew said.

"Shouldn't I call?"

"And what, tell them you forged it? No way. They'd probably take away your scholarship. Don't worry about it. I'll take care of it."

A short silence ensued.

"I'm glad you have Ryder."

Andrew's breath stilled. It was more than he'd hoped for. A boyfriend he loved, and a sister who understood. "You mean it?"

"Yeah, I do."

"Well, I'm glad, too." He squeezed her a little harder. "And I'm glad I have you again."

Andrea sighed. "Do you think Ryder will ever forgive me?"

"I'm sure he will." Andrew smiled. "Love you, Andy."

"Love you, too, Andy."

The two of them sat until the cold snow got to be too much on their backsides. They stood and brushed the snow off themselves and trudged back down the hill. When Andrew walked back inside with his sister, they were laughing with each other like they had a few weeks ago. They raced each other to the rear of the house, past their parents watching television in the living room, and ran up the stairs. Rather than going into their separate rooms, Andrea joined her brother in his.

About the Author

Jennifer Lavoie lives in Connecticut in the same city she grew up in. While growing up, she always wanted to be a writer or a teacher and briefly debated a career in marine biology. The only problem with that was she's deathly afraid of deep water. Starting during a holiday season as temporary help, she worked in a bookstore for six years and made it all the way up to assistant manager before she left to take a job teaching. Jennifer has her bachelor's degree in secondary English education and found a job in her town teaching middle school students. Along with another teacher and a handful of students, Jennifer started the first Gay-Straight Alliance at the school. She is also active in other student clubs and enjoys pairing students with books that make them love to read.

Andy Squared is her first novel.

Soliloquy Titles From Bold Strokes Books

The Secret of Othello by Sam Cameron. Florida teen detectives Steven and Denny risk their lives to search for a sunken NASA satellite—but under the waves, no one can hear you scream… (978-1-60282-742-4)

Andy Squared by Jennifer Lavoie. Andrew never thought anyone could come between him and his twin sister, Andrea… until Ryder rode into town. (978-1-60282-743-1)

Sara by Greg Herren. A mysterious and beautiful new student at Southern Heights High School stirs things up when students start dying. (978-1-60282-674-8)

Boys of Summer, edited by Steve Berman. Stories of young love and adventure, when the sky's ceiling is a bright blue marvel, when another boy's laughter at the beach can distract from dull summer jobs. (978-1-60282-663-2)

Street Dreams by Tama Wise. Tyson Rua has more than his fair share of problems growing up in New Zealand—he's gay, he's falling in love, and he's run afoul of the local hip-hop crew leader just as he's trying to make it as a graffiti artist. (978-1-60282-650-2)

me@you.com by K.E. Payne. Is it possible to fall in love with someone you've never met? Imogen Summers thinks so because it's happened to her. (978-1-60282-592-5)

Swimming to Chicago by David-Matthew Barnes. As the lives of the adults around them unravel, high school students Alex and Robby form an unbreakable bond, vowing to do anything to stay together—even if it means leaving everything behind. (978-1-60282-572-7)

Speaking Out edited by Steve Berman. Inspiring stories written for and about LGBT and Q teens of overcoming adversity (against intolerance and homophobia) and experiencing life after "coming out." (978-1-60282-566-6)

365 Days by K.E. Payne. Life sucks when you're seventeen years old and confused about your sexuality, and the girl of your dreams doesn't even know you exist. Then in walks sexy new emo girl, Hannah Harrison. Clemmie Atkins has exactly 365 days to discover herself, and she's going to have a blast doing it! (978-1-60282-540-6)

Cursebusters! by Julie Smith. Budding psychic Reeno is the most accomplished teenage burglar in California, but one tiny screw-up and poof!—she's sentenced to Bad Girl School. And that isn't even her worst problem. Her sister Haley's dying of an illness no one can diagnose, and now she can't even help. (978-1-60282-559-8)

Who I Am by M.L. Rice. Devin Kelly's senior year is a disaster. She's in a new school in a new town, and the school bully is making her life miserable—but then she meets his sister Melanie and realizes her feelings for her are more than platonic. (978-1-60282-231-3)

Sleeping Angel by Greg Herren. Eric Matthews survives a terrible car accident only to find out everyone in town thinks he's a murderer—and he has to clear his name even though he has no memories of what happened. (978-1-60282-214-6)

Mesmerized by David-Matthew Barnes. Through her close friendship with Brodie and Lance, Serena Albright learns about the many forms of love and finds comfort for the grief and guilt she feels over the brutal death of her older brother, the victim of a hate crime. (978-1-60282-191-0)

The Perfect Family by Kathryn Shay. A mother and her gay son stand hand in hand as the storms of change engulf their perfect family and the life they knew. (978-1-60282-181-1)

Father Knows Best by Lynda Sandoval. High school juniors and best friends Lila Moreno, Meryl Morganstern, and Caressa Thibodoux plan to make the most of the summer before senior year. What they discover that amazing summer about girl power, growing up, and trusting friends and family more than prepares them to tackle that all-important senior year! (978-1-60282-147-7)